THE AMAZING CHAN
GETS A ROTTEN DEAL
ON THE BROOKLYN BRIDGE

"Mr. Chan, listen," the desperate voice on the telephone had pleaded, "I want to tell you everything. Meet me tonight on the walkway of the Brooklyn Bridge."

Hours later, Charlie Chan was standing at the edge of the deserted walkway. He moved cautiously across it, unbuttoning his suit jacket so that his pistol was more readily accessible.

Suddenly Chan saw a dark car coming along the roadway. The police? Possibly, but . . . ?

The car came closer. A shotgun barrel appeared at one of its windows.

Charlie Chan did not waste time or thought on what now could not be helped. He ran for his life . . .

Bantam Books in the Charlie Chan Mystery Series
Ask your bookseller for the books you have missed

#1 THE HOUSE WITHOUT A KEY by Earl Derr Biggers
#2 THE CHINESE PARROT by Earl Derr Biggers
#3 BEHIND THAT CURTAIN by Earl Derr Biggers
#4 CHARLIE CHAN RETURNS by Dennis Lynds

Charlie Chan
Returns

**Based on a Screenplay by
Ed Spielman and Howard Friedlander
Novelization by Dennis Lynds**

BANTAM BOOKS
TORONTO · NEW YORK · LONDON

RLI: VLM 7 (VLR (6-9)
IL 7-adult

CHARLIE CHAN RETURNS
A Bantam Book / published November 1974

Bantam Books are published by Bantam Books, Inc. Its trade-
mark, consisting of the words "Bantam Books" and the por-
trayal of a bantam, is registered in the United States Patent
Office and in other countries. Marca Registrada. Bantam
Books, Inc., 666 Fifth Avenue, New York, New York 10019.

PRINTED IN THE UNITED STATES OF AMERICA

CHARLIE CHAN
RETURNS

1

That morning, the heat wave that had stifled New York in an oven for a week broke.

All through Manhattan air conditioners were switched off, and Consolidated Edison executives breathed easier as the threat of a power crisis ended for now. By 10:00 A.M. the pace of the city quickened in the clear, bright morning.

Across the East River in Long Island City, where the heat was always worse among the endless, crowded, residential blocks, streams of housewives walked the busy streets with lighter steps. At a tenth-floor window in a typical middle-class, high-rise apartment building, a man in a white shirt leaned on the sill, lazily enjoying the change in the weather.

At an hour when few men were at home in Long Island City, the man in the white shirt remained at his window for some time. His shirt still open at the collar, cuffs unbuttoned, he seemed in no hurry—a man lounging at home on a summer morning. He had an ordinary face—craggy and angular and pitted with old, acne scars—a homely face, but quiet and likeable enough. In his mid-forties, he could have been one of the thousands of office workers, mechanics, or minor executives all through the business firms of the city.

When he finally left the window and walked back into his apartment, he showed the solid walk of a stocky man just under six feet tall. The apartment was typical middle-class, full of utilitarian furniture of no special type. There were few homey touches—a bachelor's apartment, yet neat but not fussy. The man stood for a moment as if considering what to do next. He looked at his watch, and went to his front door.

Bending, he retrieved the morning paper from his doormat. He closed the door, carried the newspaper into his kitchen and laid it on a chair. He opened his refrigerator, took out a container of milk, and poured some into a bowl. As he placed the bowl on the kitchen table, a white Angora cat appeared on the table in a single, silent bound. The man watched the cat begin to lap at its breakfast, then reached out and slowly began to pet the cat.

When the cat had finished and jumped down licking at its soft whiskers, the stocky man filled a small copper watering can, and watered a row of plants on his kitchen windowsill. His few chores finished, he sat down and opened the newspaper. He sighed over the front page with all its news of the world's troubles, then turned to the inside pages. He read idly, lingering for a moment on a small story headlined: EMINENT CHINESE DETECTIVE VACATIONS IN NEW YORK CITY, and then turned to the sports pages.

He read in silence for half an hour, carefully reading all the sports stories, then looked at his watch again. He got up and went into his bedroom, put on a tie, buttoned his shirt cuffs, and took a cheap, brown suit jacket from his closet. Dressed, he studied his image in the mirror. Satisfied, he opened a bureau drawer, moved some shirts and rolled socks, and revealed an egg-shaped metal object. He picked it up lightly, with easy familiarity.

It was a hand grenade.

In the Grand Lobby of The Waldorf-Astoria Hotel on Park Avenue, the elegant guests moved briskly now that the city had been released from the grip of heat. An echo of more stately and regal times when ladies swept into rooms with flowing trains and gentlemen wore diamond stickpins, the towering lobby throbbed with a sleek efficiency as modern as any of the new glass-and-chrome hotels that were still trying to rival its eminence, yet failing.

The Waldorf was still *The* Waldorf—Number One

to anyone of importance who came to New York and demanded the best. Kings entered here, and presidents met sheiks and movie stars, so there were few who looked when a unique figure quietly entered the lobby and approached the main desk.

Trailed by two bellhops carrying his sturdy, if somewhat old, brown luggage, the man who now crossed The Waldorf's lobby was a classic figure. Dressed in a white summer suit with vest and white shoes, he had an imposing, ageless Chinese face, adorned by a neat, old-style Chinese mustache.

He carried a large, covered birdcage.

Though slightly pudgy, and not tall, there was a controlled spring to his walk that hinted at hidden power and excellent physical condition despite his quiet, reserved manner. His black hair revealed no trace of gray.

"Good morning," he spoke politely to the clerk. "You have reservation for Charlie Chan?"

The desk clerk, who had been reading the morning newspaper, jumped up quickly. He beamed at the newcomer.

"Mr. Chan! Yes, certainly," the clerk exclaimed. He shuffled swiftly through the reservation cards. "Your old suite, I'm happy to say. And may I say we're very pleased to have you with us again."

"Thank you so much," Charlie Chan said.

"It's been far too long," the clerk said, still smiling.

Chan's head bowed faintly. His slanted, black eyes, deep and intelligent, showed no emotion beyond a humorous twinkle.

"World events of many years clip wings of wandering bird," he said. "Hopping sparrow must become ostrich for a time."

"Well, we have you now. I hope you will find our best unchanged," the clerk said, and handed a key to the first bellhop. "Take Inspector Chan to suite 17-G."

With a final, faint bow, Charlie Chan turned to follow the bellhops toward the elevators. The desk clerk continued to stare admiringly after the famous detective, suddenly snapped his fingers, glanced behind him at the mail slots, and called out.

"Oh, Mr. Chan! I forgot. You have a message here!"

Chan turned back with a wry glint in his dark eyes. "Many years make few changes. What is message?"

The clerk read: "Mr. Victor Cosmo called to say he will call again at 11:00 A.M. on a matter of mutual interest."

"Victor Cosmo?" Chan's heavy eyebrows knotted severely. "Ah, so, the noted philanthropist. I have read of him."

"A fine gentleman," the clerk said. "We've had him here at many charity functions."

"Then I will await second call with pleasure," Chan said.

Chan turned once more to follow the bellhops. As he stepped into the elevator, his deep eyes were thoughtful.

Some blocks away across Manhattan, Victor Cosmo strode from the equally time-honored Plaza Hotel on the edge of Central Park. A giant of a man, he would have been called fat if his corpulence had not been matched by his tall stature. In the clear, warm sunlight he walked briskly up Fifth Avenue toward his town house.

His rich, impeccable dark suit and freshly barbered pink complexion bespoke both wealth and polish. His jaunty step and sparkling eyes revealed a cheerful man who enjoyed the world that had been very good to him. In one massive arm he cradled a multicolored bunch of three dozen roses.

A very social and gregarious man, he whistled as he strode along the sunny avenue, smiling and tipping his hat to startled strangers as he passed. His chauffeured Rolls-Royce limousine followed him at a discreet distance. The day was far too beautiful, after the recent heat wave, to ride in a closed car.

As he reached his tall town house, Cosmo waved his chauffeur away, and entered. The chic, tasteful interior of the rich house was a swirl of activity, as servants busily prepared for what could only be a dinner party. Crystal and silver were being cleaned, several maids were attending to a long, gleaming table in the vast, formal dining room, while others were dusting and shining the elegant but comfortable living room.

Victor Cosmo set his roses on the dining-room table and nodded to a maid. As she hurried forward to attend the roses, Cosmo picked up a crystal goblet. He examined it at arm's length, a small annoyance in his eyes, but without any visible frown. Polite, he held the goblet out to the maid with a gentle smile.

"Please, my dear, do this goblet once more," he said in a patient voice. "Everything must be perfect, you see."

The maid took the goblet. "Yes, Mr. Cosmo."

"Thank you, my dear."

As the maid left with the glass, Cosmo stood humming an operatic aria to himself. He glanced at a massive French marble clock on his living-room mantel, and walked to a small telephone table near the stairs. A newspaper rested on the table beside the telephone. Cosmo picked up the paper and glanced for a moment at the single-column story that had been circled on an inside page. EMINENT CHINESE DETECTIVE VACATIONS IN NEW YORK CITY. Still humming, Victor Cosmo dropped the paper on the table and reached for the telephone receiver.

In suite 17-G of The Waldorf-Astoria, Charlie Chan stood at his now uncovered birdcage. Inside the cage were two Pekin nightingales. Comfortable in his silk dressing gown, Chan spoke softly to the birds in Cantonese.

His telephone rang, making the small birds flutter inside the cylindrical cage. With a sigh Chan answered the phone. A rich voice was warm and friendly on the other end.

"Mr. Chan? Welcome to New York."

"To be welcome is always pleasant. Mr. Victor Cosmo?"

"Ah, you received my message. Let me introduce . . ."

"No need," Chan interrupted. "Victor Cosmo, diligent supporter of many charities, already introduced by magazines."

"Delightful! You flatter me greatly, Mr. Chan."

"Flattery is undeserved praise, not apply in your case," Chan said. "Most pleased you have called. But what is nature . . . ?"

"The offer, I hope, of an interesting evening, Mr. Chan," Victor Cosmo's voice said. "Forgive the short notice, but I am giving a small dinner party this evening. I have been an admirer of yours for many years, Mr. Chan, and when I read of your impending arrival, I thought that if you happened to be free tonight, you might do me the honor of attending. I believe my other guests will find you as fascinating as I think you will find them. Will you come?"

"Long trip tires one no longer as young as . . ."

"I think I can assure you my party will be most interesting," Victor Cosmo said smoothly.

Cosmo's rich voice remained as pleasant as ever, but Chan's ear detected a slight change underneath, a hint of sardonic amusement like thin steel.

"I see," Chan said. "Interesting evenings like prized pearls. I can attend. Thank you so much."

"Wonderful! It will be at eight o'clock, then. I'll leave the details with the desk. See you at eight, Mr. Chan."

The line clicked off, and Charlie Chan hung his receiver up slowly. He sat unmoving for a moment, speculation in his dark, bottomless eyes. He got up slowly and began untying his robe.

A violent knocking at his door echoed through the suite. Chan turned, startled.

"Yes, please?"

A voice answered sharply from outside the door.

"Open up in there! Police!"

2

Charlie Chan seemed to freeze in the center of the living room. His ivory face was a study in conflicting reactions—a wry distaste mixed with tolerant amusement, a reproving expression mingled with barely concealed eagerness. It was a display of feeling few people ever saw in public.

Chan moved to the door and opened it.

A dapper Chinese man in his late twenties stood at Chan's threshold. Taller than Chan and on the thin side, his horn-rimmed glasses gave him the studious appearance of an overage student. Handsome, with a happy-go-lucky manner, the visitor resembled a Chinese Cary Grant. His clothes were in fashionable good taste. Cardin sport coat, beige summer slacks, cordovan loafers.

The two men faced each other for a long moment, both smiling. Then, without hesitation or embarrassment, they threw their arms around each other. However, as if suddenly discomfited by the display of emotion, Chan disengaged himself, drew the younger man into the suite, and closed the door. He stood back and studied his visitor.

"Number Three son most pleasant sight," Chan said quietly. "How have you been, 'Hotshot'?"

"Hello, Pop," Jimmy Chan said. "I've missed you."

"Please," Chan said with a mock frown. "Save wild sentiment for semiannual letter to your mother."

"Sure, Pop," Jimmy grinned.

"You look well," Chan said, and continued to examine his third son. "But you have gained weight?"

"A couple of pounds."

"Good," Chan said, looking up at Jimmy's head. "But your hair is too long."

"Got to swing with the times, right?" Jimmy laughed. "So tell me all about things at home."

Still grinning, Jimmy took off his jacket and threw it on a chair. Chan stared at his son, his heavy eyebrows rising in a kind of amused curiosity. Under his jacket Jimmy Chan wore a belt holster that carried a snub-nosed, .357 Colt Magnum pistol fitted with custom grips, and a shoulder holster containing a .38-cal. Beretta automatic. Charlie Chan blinked.

"Jimmy," Chan said. "Second World War is over. Fact well known. Recall—*we won!*"

Jimmy looked down at his private arsenal. Casual and relaxed, he was so familiar with his dual hardware that he appeared to have forgotten he was wearing the guns. He shrugged. Chan seemed to shake his head over such heavy weaponry.

"Number Three son must wear such heavy iron?"

"Only if I want to go out, Pop," Jimmy said wryly. "A cop in this town makes a lot of enemies."

"Fact not confined to New York," Chan said. "Sometimes is an asset. One can tell character of a man by the enemies he must make."

"In this town they come out of the woodwork in all shapes and sizes," Jimmy said, shaking his head. "It's different here now than in your early days, Pop."

"Perhaps," Chan said. "But son not come to talk shop with ancient detective. You are free for lunch?"

"Sorry, Pop. How about dinner?"

"Regret, have foolishly made dinner engagement."

"Well," Jimmy said. "We can talk a while now, and I'll take my day off to show you around *my* town."

"May not survive such excitement," Chan said dryly.

Jimmy laughed again, and then looked thoughtful, his face almost a miniature of his father's. "How come you've got a dinner date so soon? You just arrived, and you like to stay alone the first night. Got a hot date?"

"Engagement with prominent male, temperature not

stated," Chan said. "Only that evening will be interesting."

"I've heard that one before. Usually means a dull bummer."

"Most probable," Chan agreed. "Still, when farmer invite fox to dinner, possible he have chicken to frighten."

"You think someone wants a famous detective . . .?"

"Speculation idle exercise," Chan said. "Father and son have better to talk about. You wish to hear of home? Know that youngest sister smile at last without mouth of silver. She . . ."

Jimmy grinned again as he listened to Chan's tale of home, and the subject of the evening's dinner was forgotten.

In the Broadway office of a famous theatrical agent, Victor Cosmo's party wasn't forgotten. The agent, a pale and nervous little man with the permanently sweating palms of his trade, watched a stately, dark-haired woman pace up and down his expensive carpet.

"Oh, God, must I really go? Still a command performance when Victor invites?"

"Cosmo is still a big power, Lorraine," the agent said.

"Damn it, I don't need him now!"

"But you owe him, and people remember," the agent said. "Besides, an actress never knows when she'll need a rich backer again, does she?"

Lorraine McCall swore—good, solid swearing that would have startled the millions of popcorn-eating fans who paid to see her world-famous films. It didn't fit her image. In her forties now, she looked many years younger, with a dark and stately beauty she worked hard to maintain. A decent actress, but it was her self-possessed beauty and charismatic bearing that the viewers paid to see. Elegant and regal—that was her image—and it didn't go with a soldier-of-fortune vocabulary. But the real-life hint of hardness under the facade did.

"Oh, damn, alright!" she cried with the famous

patrician toss of her long, dark hair. "I only hope Victor's invited *some* interesting people besides me. He's become such a bore."

The agent didn't even sigh. He was used to it by now.

Lorraine McCall's words were repeated like a delayed echo one hour later in a midtown art gallery. The speaker of the identical sentiment was a small, slender man with darkish, Mediterranean skin and sharp, Levantine eyes.

"Victor is a bore, *fini!*" the small man said flatly to the gallery owner. "They come to his parties, the dull people, to look at *me*—Lalique! Who could rival me, eh?"

"A lot are trying," the gallery owner said dryly. "Art changes fast these days, Lalique. Yesterday's genius, can be . . ."

The small man bristled and stared unblinking at the gallery owner. The renowned painter wore a black satin suit and carried a delicate ivory cane—one of the hundreds of bizarre costumes that were his trademark. In his right eye he wore a rose-colored monocle that hid nothing of the venom of his stare. He seemed to rise taller in anger, a slim bundle of enormous conceit.

"You dare suggest Lalique has any rival?" he said softly.

"No, not Lalique," the gallery owner said mildly. He lit a cigarette and stared back at the painter unintimidated. "But your work does. People are saying it's becoming erratic, varying too much. They're resisting your prices. That's cold fact, my friend, genuine coin of the realm."

Lalique changed suddenly. He smiled. It was a sinister smile, like a Cheshire cat, his perfectly capped teeth very white against his dark skin.

"Then lower the prices—a little," he said and shrugged. "Business is business."

"I already have," the owner said. "A little. Go to Victor Cosmo's party. Be outrageous. Be Lalique, eh? Drop your pants for some blue-blood lady at the dinner table. Prices will go up again."

Both men smiled, then laughed aloud. Lalique twirled his ivory cane, and winked behind his rose-colored monocle.

The man who pushed his way out of City Hall, brushing aside the reporters on his way to a black limousine, was not smiling or laughing. Jeffrey Lowman, *enfant terrible* of New York Reform politics and front-running potential candidate for mayor, got into the limousine without a backward glance, and ordered his chauffeur to drive to Battery Park.

As the big car glided smoothly through the heavy downtown lunch-hour traffic, Jeffrey Lowman sat back scowling. A tall, slim man in his mid-thirties, he wore a reserved, Ivy League dark suit and vest, with a Phi Beta Kappa key from Harvard hanging from a watch chain. His prep-school haircut and scholarly glasses covered a sharp mind and aggressive personality. His fingers drummed and his foot tapped as he rode toward the river.

"Battery Park, sir," the chauffeur said. "Any special . . . ?"

"Just wait here," Lowman said curtly.

Lowman walked along the edge of the river, wide here in the bright noontime sun, until he was out of sight of the limousine. Then he turned away from the river and walked quickly through the park thronged with office workers from the nearby tall buildings of Lower Manhattan. No one seemed to recognize him. He was vaguely annoyed as he left the park, but the feeling passed quickly. Lowman stopped at a crowded corner as if deciding which way to walk. A short, heavy businessman stopped near him.

"I can't meet you tonight," Lowman said.

"It's important," the short man said, looking away idly.

"Victor Cosmo is giving a party. I have to go."

"Yeh?" the short man said. "Someday, you'll have to make up your mind—him or us."

"No, I won't," Jeffrey Lowman said. "I'm going to be mayor."

He walked toward the park without looking back.

Naked, Winston Cleaver came out of his bathroom. A small, stocky, fleshy man with pink skin like a flabby baby, he stood drying himself delicately, smiling at the half-hidden figure lying in his bed under the sheets. Cleaver's voice was caressing.

"I'll see you again, dear, won't I? Tomorrow?"

The figure moved and giggled. "Why not tonight, lover?"

"Sorry, not tonight. Victor is offering dinner."

Half-amused, Cleaver went on drying his soft, pink flesh as though he liked to touch himself. But his flabby, middle-aged gaze and tiny eyes were suddenly annoyed. His look became petulant, like a fat, sinister teddy bear.

"I'd rather stay with you," he said to the bed, "but . . ."

"But," the figure in bed said, "Victor is important."

The figure sat up, reached for a cigarette, lit it, and sat back against the elegant headboard. He smoked and smiled. Naked above the sheets, his broad, young chest showed wisps of curling blond hair. In his early twenties, he smoked with the cigarette dangling at the corner of his mouth. A clean-cut youth with strong shoulders, he flexed his biceps at Cleaver.

"Careful, Winnie," he said, "I may not be here tomorrow."

"Don't say that!" Cleaver almost whined.

"Me or Victor Cosmo," the youth said.

"Victor is the only Victor," Cleaver snapped, his small eyes icy. "You I can find in any gay bar!"

"You know, you could at that," the young man said.

Winston dropped the towel and hurried toward the bed. "I'm sorry, Donnie. I didn't mean that. But Victor . . ."

The boy went on smoking.

Jimmy Chan walked out of The Waldorf into the noontime sun, and climbed into a waiting, unmarked, black police cruiser. His partner, Norbitz, slid over and let Jimmy take the wheel.

"How's your old man?" Norbitz asked.

"He's great," Jimmy said, and smiled almost to himself. "The same old Charlie Chan. I'll spend my day off with him."

"Not tonight? How come?"

"He's got a dinner to go to. He . . ."

Jimmy's voice slowly faded away as he stared mesmerized at his partner. Norbitz was a heavy-set, bull of a man of thirty-four. Prematurely balding, with hairy knuckles and a definite potbelly despite his muscle, Norbitz looked like he slept in his suit—a sloppy, rumpled bear compared to Jimmy Chan's dapper neatness. But it wasn't his partner's appearance that made Jimmy slowly speechless.

Norbitz was eating a hot dog—complete with mustard, onions, sauerkraut, relish, ketchup and piccalilli! "Eating" was probably the wrong word. Hungry, Norbitz was devouring the frank in gargantuan bites.

"Don't you know that stuff'll kill you?" Jimmy said when he finally got his voice back. "You know what's in one of those? Chemicals, chicken beaks and insect parts. Ugh!"

Ignoring Jimmy, Norbitz ate on, swallowed the last bite, and wiped his mouth with his hand. He looked at Jimmy for a moment, then leaned out the window toward the frankfurter vendor.

"Hey! Gimme another frank—the works!"

Norbitz leaned back and grinned at Jimmy Chan. "Hey, maybe your old man likes hot dogs? Maybe he gets franks for dinner?"

"Yuk," Jimmy said. "He'd rather have poison."

In Long Island City, the solitary man with the acne-scarred face walked along the almost-deserted early afternoon streets. He carried a bag of groceries, picked up his mail as he entered his building, and rode up to his apartment.

Inside, he set the groceries on a table and held a fat envelope. He opened it and removed a thick stack of money—all hundred dollar bills. He held the money irreverently, bent and held it out to the Angora cat that rubbed at his legs. Then he carelessly tossed the money onto the table and watched the bills flutter.

As he observed the scattered money, something

seemed to happen to his face. Expressionless on the surface, there was something underneath. Something cold and manic, yet detached. Not something *there* in his eyes, but something *missing*—some element of normal people that had been left out of this man.

Quietly, as if suddenly drawn by an unseen voice, the man went into his bedroom, opened the bureau drawer and took out the hand grenade. He carried it almost lovingly into the kitchen as if it were part of him. From the bag of groceries he took out two boxes of shotgun shells. He placed these beside the grenade on the table, and stood looking down at his arsenal.

3

The lights of Victor Cosmo's town house spilled out into the springlike night of the Upper East Side. The crowds who passed on the street seemed to stare up in envy. Charlie Chan, arriving by taxi, stopped for a moment to study the imposing house. Then he rang, and was admitted by a maid.

"Charlie Chan, please," he announced quietly.

"Go right in, Mr. Chan."

Bowing, Chan turned through the immaculate foyer toward the clear sound of animated voices in the mansion living room. At the doorway, he paused again to observe the glittering scene. The room was large and rich. The knot of guests in evening clothes was small, but they were people with the power to dominate any room. Most dominant of all was Victor Cosmo himself, a diamond gleaming beneath his white tie in the brilliant light.

"Ah, Mr. Chan!" the philanthropist cried, seeing the detective. "Come in, come in!"

All heads in the room turned as Chan entered. Victor Cosmo advanced toward the detective with outstretched hand, a startlingly beautiful young woman clinging to his other arm.

"So good of you to come. I am Victor Cosmo."

Chan bowed. "Most honored."

"It is I who am honored," Victor Cosmo said, bowing in return.

Chan looked politely toward the stunning blonde at Victor Cosmo's side. Her alabaster face had faultless features. Her eyes were green, and her blonde hair was

15

set in a stylish French cut. A model's face and beauty
—too posed and too perfect, like an ornament turned
out by a master craftsman. Her green eyes were wide
but empty, a vapid face. Seeing Chan's glance, Victor
Cosmo flicked his wrist toward the girl without looking
at her.

"My, ah, associate, Mr. Chan. Natalie, a most stylish
model, don't you think?"

"Of great beauty," Chan said, smiling at the girl.

Cosmo flicked his wrist again. "My dear, get a drink
for Mr. Chan."

"A small glass of wine, perhaps," Chan said.

The fabulous blonde walked away toward the corner bar. Victor Cosmo took Chan's arm and turned
toward his other guests. He raised his voice loudly.

"Everyone! I want you all to meet our final guest.
Mr. Charlie Chan!" Cosmo paused, smiled. "The famous detective!"

Cosmo went on smiling as a silence seemed to hang
over the brightly-lit room. Chan's eyes narrowed faintly, but the silence was broken almost at once by a
small, flabby man with the pink face of a teddy bear
in evening clothes.

"Are we all under arrest, Victor?" Winston Cleaver
asked, his voice languid with bored amusement as he
eyed Chan.

"No, Winston," Victor Cosmo said curtly, his smile
thin and cutting now. "They don't arrest people like
you anymore."

Winston Cleaver flushed like an overage girl, but
Cosmo's smile broadened again immediately, and he
turned to Chan.

"I would suspect that all my guests are known to
you, Mr. Chan?" the philanthropist said.

Before Chan could answer, the stunning blonde,
Natalie, returned with his glass of wine. Chan took the
glass with a gracious nod, sipped it appreciatively, and
then turned toward a tall, dark, stately woman in a
sleek, silver evening dress.

"Most difficult not to recognize great film actress
Lorraine McCall," he said.

The actress raised her glass to Chan, acknowledging

his compliment with an open, ingratiating smile. Chan turned next to the small, languid Winston Cleaver.

"Mr. Winston Cleaver, of course," the detective said. "Writer of excellent mystery novels."

Cleaver forced a smile. "I must say I'm surprised, Mr. Chan. As a rule, almost no one knows a writer's face. We are invisible people."

"Fortunately I have curious habit," Chan said. "Always read back of book jacket, observe photograph of author."

"Ah? It seems your reputation as a detective is no fable, eh, Inspector Chan?" Cleaver remarked easily.

Chan's bow was good-natured. Victor Cosmo, observing all that went on, waved now to the tall, clean-cut man in front of a marble fireplace who wore his white-tie and tails as if born to them.

"And, of course," Cosmo said, "I'm sure you know our Reform hope, Jeffrey Lowman."

"Soon to be candidate for mayor," Chan said, stepping toward the handsome politician. "Pleased to make acquaintance of man who wish thankless task of saving great city."

With a reserved nod Jeffrey Lowman shook Chan's proffered hand, and returned to his position against the mantelpiece. He said nothing, and Chan turned lastly to the small, slender, dark man in a black satin suit and bizarre, rose-colored monocle.

"And Lalique, world-famous artist," Chan said. "An honor."

"*Bien,* Mr. Chan, and thank you," Lalique purred, and held up his glass in salute. "But not simply famous. No, not Lalique. Supreme! The ultimate artist! Lalique *is* art. The two are synonymous, interchangeable! There is not one without the other."

Chan's voice was without flattery. "Foremost art critics have similar opinion," he said.

"Ah!" Lalique was delighted. "Then you *know* art, Mr. Chan? Fascinating! Fate has planned for us to meet, *hein?* As simple people collect stamps, Lalique collects greatness. I have long known that master criminals and great detectives are artists in their own right. While your level of genuis is not so lofty as my own, nevertheless Lalique respects you as a man of genuis!"

"Thank you," Chan said dryly. "Am most complimented."

"So, we have all met," Victor Cosmo beamed around the great room. "Now I believe it is time for dinner."

As if on signal, a maid opened the door into the dining room, revealing the long table gleaming with crystal and silver. Victor Cosmo waved his massive hand.

"Shall we?"

Offering his arm to Lorraine McCall, Chan entered the dining room amid a rising buzz of conversation. But the detective's dark eyes narrowed as he proceeded to the table. For all the smiles and conversation, he sensed that there was little warmth to the gathering, rather an undercurrent of tension.

With the arrival of coffee and liqueurs, Charlie Chan sat back at the long table, still savoring the excellent French cuisine. As the diners placed their damask napkins on the table and sat in more comfortable positions to enjoy their coffee and after-dinner drinks, the servants left the long room.

The doors closed, as if on previous instructions, and the guests glanced around. A sense of isolation descended on the room, the undercurrent of tension suddenly surfacing like a deadly undersea reef. Jeffrey Lowman half rose.

"Victor, I thank you . . ."

Cosmo shook his head gently, a small smile on his massive face. He sat there for a moment. When he finally spoke, all attention focused on him, his smooth voice was most amiable.

"The time has come for me, as host, to say the immortal words—'you may have wondered why you were all invited here tonight.' " He beamed at his guests. "Perhaps you actually did wonder why I made it clear you were to come without escorts?"

Winston Cleaver shrugged. "I can imagine why you didn't want an escort of mine here, Victor. You are quite prudish."

"No," Cosmo said shaking his head. "You are wrong,

Winston. I made the condition simply because I thought this gathering should be of a very private nature. With the obvious exception of Mr. Chan, I have known all of you for many years."

Lorraine McCall laughed. "Auld lang syne, Victor?"

"Touché, my dear," Cosmo said, still benign. "But you are not quite correct. As I said, I have known each of you a very long time—and our relationship has greatly benefited each other!" His smile faded slowly. "In fact, you are all my creatures."

The buzz was low but angry in the bright room. Victor Cosmo waited. His smile was gone now, and with it his benign manner. He waved a hand harshly, a sudden malignance in his eyes.

"For instance," he glanced at Lalique, "to look at him, and to hear him, one would never suspect that Lalique is, in reality, a man of the most *minor* artistic talent."

The little painter went white. "What are you saying?"

"Merely the truth," Victor Cosmo said calmly. "If it weren't for me, Lalique would be a nonentity today."

"You're a liar!" Lalique cried.

"No, little man," Cosmo snapped coldly. *"You are a fraud!"* He fixed the bizarre painter with his eyes. "For years you have been signing your name to works which other artists have created under my patronage!"

In an electric silence, Lalique's rose-colored monocle had dropped from his eye. It swung against his satin suit that suddenly seemed sleazy. The slender painter didn't seem to notice the lost monocle.

"Admit it," Victor Cosmo said. "Admit it to the others."

The gaudy painter licked his lips, his dark, Levantine face furtive, but he said nothing.

"Very refreshing," Victor Cosmo said with disgust. "For once Lalique has nothing to say."

With those cutting words, the last pretense of civility vanished from the room. Venom flowed through the charged air. Jeffrey Lowman studied his dinner knife, the rising politician's firm voice coming out low and quiet.

"Is there some point to all this, Victor?"

"Point?" Cosmo's eyebrows went up. "Why, certainly there is a point, Mr. *Mayor*," he said ironically. "Everything I do is premeditated. That is one thing we have in common, Jeffrey."

"We have nothing in common," Jeffrey Lowman said.

Cosmo shook his imposing head. "Let us not be naive, Jeffrey. Your rise to political position and power has been directly attributable to two factors: first, I have bankrolled your campaigns, and second, your loyalties have always been for sale to the highest bidder." The philanthropist sighed. "You are a political whore, Jeffrey. As the darling of the Reform movement, you leave much to be desired."

Lowman flushed, but maintained a stony silence. Lalique still sat as if stunned, and Lorraine McCall fought to keep a thin smile on her patrician face, the fear gone out of her eyes. The beautiful blonde, Natalie, stared down at her empty plate, obviously confused and embarrassed. Chan watched them all with an alert, wary fascination, as they flinched under the derisive attack of the vitriolic Victor Cosmo.

Unexpectedly, it was the pink and flabby Winston Cleaver who refused to quail before their sardonic host.

"Victor," Cleaver said calmly, "you are truly a Prince of Swine."

"Ah," Cosmo said softly, "my little mother's helper. So we come to you? As a writer, I cannot fault you ..."

"Thank you," Cleaver snapped, "for nothing."

"Provided," Victor Cosmo continued, "one has a taste for your moronic little mystery stories. However, for years your bedroom antics with anyone, from sailors to hoodlums, have been a great embarrassment to me."

"Embarrassment, Victor?" the writer shot back. "You're not capable of it. That trait is reserved for human beings. As for my personal life, it is none of your business."

"Really? Why, Winston, how many times have you called me, shrieking for me to advance you money to bail you out of one of your little 'problems'? How many times have I soothed the vice squad for you? What efforts have I gone to so that your 'good name' would be kept out of the scandal sheets? If it weren't for me, *dear,* your writing would be confined to the walls of men's rooms—or prison cells!"

Quietly, with a certain dignity, Cleaver stood up. "The party's over, Victor."

"Sit down!"

Victor Cosmo's bellow shook the room, rattling the crystal and silver with frightening rage. The guests seemed transfixed, as the philanthropist dominated them like a predator over its prey.

"I'm not through quite yet," he said, and looked at Lorraine McCall.

"My turn, Victor?" the dark-haired actress asked.

"I won't disappoint you, my dear," Cosmo purred, and produced a small reel of 8-mm film from his tailcoat pocket. He held the reel up for all to see. "Do you know what this is, Lorraine? Some of your finest early footage."

Sudden fear crossed Lorraine McCall's face like a slap.

"I think," Victor Cosmo toyed with her, "our guests would find this little 'classic' infinitely more entertaining than your latest film. Certainly more *revealing,* eh?"

"Where did you get that?" the actress cried.

"Oh, there are still a few collectors' copies around. Old, but, ah, stimulating." Cosmo addressed his guests. "This film is from Lorraine's *experimental* youth. Tell our guests what type of film it is, Lorraine. What kind of experiments such an aristocratic *lady* performed for the camera once. Tell them how you started in motion pictures before I met you. If you won't, I'll show them." He turned to Natalie. "My dear, ask one of the servants to get my projector."

Knocking her chair flying, Lorraine McCall was up on her feet. She snatched a knife from the table, her classic face in contorted fury, and leaped at Victor Cosmo. The steel-bladed knife plunged downward at Victor Cosmo—and stopped in midair. Charlie Chan, moving with a quickness unexpected in such a calm, stout man, caught the actress's wrist and took the knife away.

Lorraine McCall collapsed, sobbing.

Cosmo hadn't moved a hair through it all. He sat unmoving like an encompassing Buddha. Slowly, he began to unwind the roll of film in his hands, holding a strip up to the light.

"Such a fuss over a reel of blank film," he said.

Cosmo smiled, amused by his trick to bait Lorraine McCall. Still sobbing, the actress looked up at the fat man.

"You're sick, Victor," she said.

Before the philanthropist could answer, Chan spoke.

"Must echo words of Mr. Lowman—is there point to this?"

Victor Cosmo nodded and stood up. He walked to a side table where a cassette recorder stood ready.

"Yes, Mr. Chan, there is a point." Cosmo's voice was serious now. "In yesterday's mail I received something which has disturbed me greatly, and for good reason."

He switched on the cassette recorder. The tape that sounded through the room had been constructed from separate words, each in a different voice, pitch and tone.

"Dear—Victor—for—all—of—the—pain—which—you—have—delighted—in—inflicting—upon—others—you—are—going—to—die—it—will—be—very—soon—wait—to—die—Victor."

As the sinister message ended, an interminable silence seemed to hang over the brilliant room.

4

As the silent tape continued to turn, rasping only static, Charlie Chan seemed almost asleep, his impassive expression unwavering. But his dark, hooded eyes were taking careful note of the six faces around him in the tense dining room.

Victor Cosmo slowly turned off the recorder. He turned to face Chan.

"It would appear, Mr. Chan, that one of my honored guests here tonight is planning to murder me."

There was a sudden buzz of protest in the room, all the guests hurrying to deny the accusation at the same time.

"*Someone* at least wish to frighten," Chan said. "Roaring lion not always have claws, and can potential victim be certain enemies confined to present guests?"

Winston Cleaver said, "Your line of enemies must reach to a few miles beyond the moon, dear Victor."

"Perhaps you counted on that assumption, Winston?" Victor Cosmo said. He shook his head. "No, I have thought it over in great detail. There are only you four with enough motive or hate to kill me. I have helped greatly to make each of you a success, I can ruin each of you just as easily, and I have outlived my usefulness to you. I am despised by all four, and no longer needed. I know too much, and I remind you of what you all once were."

"You're hated, Victor," Winston Cleaver said cheerfully, "for no other reason than that you use people as if they were toilet tissue."

"Possibly all you are good for," Victor Cosmo returned. "In any event, you four are the only ones who would enjoy sending me a tape like that. It achieved some of its purpose—it gave me one sleepless night. There will be no more such nights, and I will *not* be murdered by such jackals!"

The massive man fixed them with his eyes and smiled confidently. "So, I have taken several precautions. I have recorded my transactions with each of you in a ledger. Should its contents be made public, the next morning each and every one of you would be ruined before nightfall—finished! What I have written in detail is in no way as 'mild' as what you heard tonight."

Cosmo paused to let them think about that for a time, then he nodded toward Charlie Chan.

"Furthermore, I took the opportunity to invite Mr. Chan to these proceedings. Should I be found dead, Mr. Chan is now aware of all the suspects. You know his reputation, you know that it would be impossible for you to evade him."

The fat host sat down, lit a long, Russian cigarette, and leaned back easily. "So you see, there is no point in my worrying, is there? You may all hate me enough to kill, but each of you has too much to live for to risk being caught for murder. I will survive many full years longer." He smiled a wolfish smile now. "Survival is the art of the unexpected."

He seemed to wait for some response, but there was none. They all watched him and, abruptly, a cloud seemed to cross his heavy face as if he were intolerably annoyed. He stood up and tossed his napkin onto the table.

"So now the party *is* over. I bid you each good night."

Instantly, as if again on signal, the servants appeared through the doors carrying hats and evening wraps. In silence, with as much haste as their host, the four "old friends" of Victor Cosmo made their exits into the cool, summer night. Chan was the last to reach the foyer. Victor Cosmo followed him out of the party rooms.

"I can imagine your distaste at having been 'used,' Mr. Chan," the philanthropist said. "I apologize humbly, but I felt I had no choice."

"Evening most educational," Chan said, obviously piqued, but thoughtful. "But strongly suggest you report death threat to police."

"Bah! I have drawn their teeth, Mr. Chan." The philanthropist appeared unperturbed, even smug. "I thought I handled it rather well."

"Possible, but be most careful, Mr. Cosmo," Chan said slowly. "Simple matter to pick up cobra, more difficult to put down unbitten."

"Your concern is flattering, Mr. Chan," Victor Cosmo said, but his eyes turned to follow the slim, feminine curves of Natalie as she went up the stairs toward the bedrooms.

It was over an hour later that Victor Cosmo rose from the giant, circular bed where Natalie's nude body lay half-covered among the rumpled sheets. She watched the fat man with warm, sensual eyes. Cosmo smiled thinly, cinched the cord of his silk robe around his enormous waist, and left the blonde model's bedroom without another word.

In the silent corridor of his mansion, Cosmo paused to look back at Natalie's door. He glanced at his watch, then walked quickly, for such a fat man, up the circular stairs to his own bedroom. He threw off his robe, turned on a small stereo radio, and strode into the bathroom. On the sink he laid out various expensive toiletries and lotions, the unguents of a man who took very good care of himself.

For a moment he looked into his bathroom mirror, then slowly broke into a satisfied smile—a smile that was very close to a knowing laugh, as he reached into the frosted glass enclosure of his shower stall to turn on the hot water.

Clouds of steam rose up as Cosmo stepped quickly into the shower like a man in a hurry.

In suite 17-G of The Waldorf-Astoria, Charlie Chan uncovered his Pekin nightingales as he entered, spoke quietly to them in Cantonese, then walked to the telephone.

"Lieutenant Chan, please," he said into the receiver.

"I'm sorry, sir, Lieutenant Chan is out on a call. If you tell me what you want, I can contact the . . ."

"Must speak with Lieutenant in person, most urgent. Please to contact quickly as possible. Have Lieutenant call Inspector Charlie Chan."

"Oh, is this Inspector Chan, his father? I'll . . ."

"Family connection of no importance now, matter of perhaps impending homicide. Make great effort."

"Right away, Inspector."

Slowly, Chan hung up, his dark eyes uneasy.

In his steaming shower, Victor Cosmo reached for his scented soap—and froze. On the wall above the frosted partition of the stall, two words had been daubed in black shoe polish.

"Good-bye, Victor"

Frantic, Victor Cosmo's wild eyes searched the inside of the shower stall. Through the billowing steam, his horrified eyes saw the hand grenade. It was taped to a corner of the shower stall, its triggering mechanism released when the shower door was closed.

Victor Cosmo clawed at the stall door.

He didn't make it.

The grenade exploded with a shattering blast, the bathroom disintegrated.

Natalie sat bolt upright in her bed. The explosion still seemed to shake the house. Staring wildly, she seized her robe, and ran out into the corridor without waiting to put it on.

She stumbled up the circular staircase and into Victor Cosmo's bedroom. Smoke and dust still drifted out of what had once been the bathroom door. Hysterical, Natalie picked her way through the wreckage to the bathroom.

She looked inside—and dropped her robe in horror.

Naked, blood and shattered debris around her, the beautiful blonde began to scream and scream.

5

In the late Victor Cosmo's bedroom and shattered bathroom, police photographers popped their flash-bulbs, and teams of technicians combed the wreckage. Uniformed patrolmen kept the curious out and the reporters in line. Chan and Jimmy stood near the bathroom. Norbitz came out of the shambles, brushing dust from the sleeve of his suit.

"Got anything?" Jimmy asked his bull-like partner.

"Yeah, a pain in the ass," Norbitz said. He shrugged, looking back at the bathroom. "Nothin'."

"What about the body?" Jimmy said.

"What body?" Norbitz said. "There ain't enough to put in a shopping bag."

Jimmy shuddered. "What was it? Dynamite? Plastic?"

"Hand grenade," Norbitz said. "Fragmentation type. Taped to a corner of the shower stall down low, right where the glass door slid back when open. Pin out, the arming handle up against the edge of the sliding panel to hold it in. When Cosmo slid the door shut the pressure released, the arming handle flew off, and she blew in five seconds. Nice. Killer knew what he was doing."

"Charming," Jimmy said.

"Sure," Norbitz agreed. "Even left Cosmo a love note, or someone did. Take a look."

Jimmy and Chan looked into the bathroom where police experts were knee-deep in debris. The front of the shower stall was completely blown away. Norbitz pointed up to the wall behind the shower. Chunks of

27

tile had disintegrated, but the two words, *"Good-bye, Victor,"* were still legible.

Jimmy and Norbitz walked away to where Natalie sat on the bed, dressed only in her bathrobe. Chan remained at the bathroom door for a moment, his half-closed eyes contemplating the remains of the scrawled message.

On the bed, Natalie's hands trembled, and her perfect face was drained of color. She seemed in a state of shock. Norbitz looked her up and down without expression, as if judging a prize cut of meat that didn't especially make him hungry.

A patrolman walked up to Jimmy Chan.

"All the windows and doors are locked from inside, Lieutenant. No sign of forced entry."

"Okay, Panzarella," Jimmy said. "Take a look around outside, will you?"

"Sure," Patrolman Panzarella said. "You oughta see the garden he got back there. Me, all I got is weeds and concrete out in Queens."

"At least you can still see the weeds," Jimmy said.

"Yeh, you got something there."

Panzarella went out, and Jimmy turned back to Natalie. As he and Norbitz began to question the model, Chan wandered casually around the room, nosing into corners, examining everything. He seemed oblivious to the bustle in the rooms, or the questioning of Jimmy and Norbitz—an unassuming shadow. But if anyone had observed closely, they would have noticed that the master detective was, somehow, always within earshot of the questioning.

"Miss . . . uh . . ." Jimmy began.

"Natalie," Norbitz said. "Just Natalie, you know? I mean, she only uses one name. She's a model—she says."

"Okay, Natalie," Jimmy said. "There are no signs of anyone breaking into the house. Is there any other way for someone to get in here unseen?"

"No," the blonde said, softly. "I . . . I don't see how."

Norbitz said, "Did you let anyone in?"

"No!" Natalie blinked up at him. "Of course not."

"No one?" Norbitz insisted. "You're sure?"

She shook her head vaguely. "It's . . . it's so hard to think. There were deliveries all day for Victor's party, yes. But . . . but they're always taken at the door. Victor is . . . was very strict about that. I'm sure . . ." She looked up at both Jimmy and Norbitz. "Victor didn't like strangers in the house, you see."

"What about the servants?" Jimmy asked.

"They've been with Victor for years. They're very loyal."

"Okay," Jimmy said, "tell me again about the party. Did anyone come upstairs? Even for a brief time? Especially *before* my fath . . . Inspector Chan arrived?"

"No one," Natalie said. "Not that I can remember. Of course, I was with Victor, I wasn't looking all the time."

Jimmy and Norbitz let the implications of that hang in the bustling room.

"What was your relationship to Mr. Cosmo?" Jimmy said instead. "You were his wife, maybe?"

Natalie looked down. "No, I just live here."

"You mean you lived with Cosmo," Norbitz said bluntly. "His roommate like, real steady."

"Yes," Natalie said.

Jimmy said, "How were you getting along lately?"

"Getting along?" She seemed puzzled. "He was a lot older than me, you know, but we . . ." She stopped, her eyes widening as she understood the insinuation. "We got along fine! You hear? Fine!"

"I was just curious," Jimmy said blandly.

"Victor was very good to me!"

"Yeah," Norbitz said. "Sure."

Natalie turned on the balding partner. "Just what are you trying to say?"

"Look, lady," Norbitz said, "no one came up here, the doors and windows are locked. You were the only one we know about with access to Cosmo's bathroom, and he ends up taking a shower with a hand grenade. You tell me what I'm trying to say!"

Natalie stared up with shocked eyes, and suddenly dissolved in tears. She cried and shook her head back and forth in violent denial and grief. While Jimmy and Norbitz watched, a sardonic smile on Norbitz's face as if saying he'd seen better performances, but Natalie's wasn't bad, Patrolman Panzarella came up carrying a small evening purse.

"Found this in the bushes out back," Panzarella said.

"That's mine!" Natalie cried.

Jimmy took the purse and handed it to the girl. "Check it to see if anything's missing."

Drying her eyes while Norbitz watched cynically, Natalie took the purse and rummaged through it.

"Everything seems to be here," she said. "Money, credit cards, handkerchief, my cigarettes . . ."

Chan turned toward them. As if his movement were a magnet, they all looked at the eminent detective. Chan nodded to Natalie.

"Please," he said mildly, "check for keys to house."

"Keys?" She blinked, then searched the purse. "Why, they're not here! My keys are gone!"

Chan looked unsurprised. "So much for means of entry."

"Hell!" Norbitz said.

Chan queried Natalie, "When was last time you saw purse?"

"Just before the first guest came," the blonde said firmly. "I *really* remember, because I'd just checked my face in my compact mirror when Mr. Lowman arrived. I was in the foyer, and I dropped my purse on the foyer table."

"Lowman saw you drop the purse?" Norbitz said.

Jimmy said, "Pop . . . !"

"Useless fact," Chan said. "Any of guests could have seen purse in plain sight in foyer, and guessed lady of house would have keys. I myself observed purse now that I recall."

Jimmy was excited. "That would mean that someone took the keys, and came back *after* the party to plant the grenade. That should narrow it down when we check their movements after leaving here!"

"Possible," Chan agreed. "But also possible killer gain entry earlier. Many ways for clever man in house where party is being prepared. Method of crime suggest knowledge of weapons on part of killer, perhaps even suggest hired professional."

"Okay, sure," Jimmy said. "But one of the guests *could* have taken the keys and returned, as long as the servants didn't spot him, and Cosmo was out of his room long enough."

"The servants were all busy cleaning up," Natalie said uneasily. "The foyer can't be seen from the dining room."

"And," Chan said, "was Victor Cosmo out of own bedroom long enough for killer to plant weapon?"

Natalie flushed. "Yes, he was."

"How long, please?" Chan said quietly.

"An hour . . . at least," the blonde said, softly.

Norbitz whistled, grinning. "Hey, quite a guy."

"He *was!*" Natalie said with a defiant toss of her blonde hair. "He had *finesse,* he never liked to rush anything."

"Nice," Norbitz said, still grinning at the lush girl.

Natalie stood up angrily. "Can I go now, Mr. Chan?"

"Alright," Jimmy said. "Go ahead, but stay around."

The blonde turned, holding her robe tightly closed as she passed Norbitz who went on grinning at her. Chan held up his hand.

"One moment, please," Chan said. "At party, Victor Cosmo referred to ledger recording his transactions with those present. You know whereabouts of this ledger?"

"No," Natalie said. "I'd never heard of it before."

They watched the slender, lush girl walk out of the bedroom, her firm body clear under the robe. Norbitz stared after her in admiration. Jimmy turned to Chan.

"What's this about a ledger, Pop?"

Chan explained Victor Cosmo's precaution to them. His ivory face was solemn behind its old-fashioned mustache.

"Jimmy, Norbitz," he said, "ledger must be found, or murders may have just begun."

6

At the moment Charlie Chan was warning Jimmy and Norbitz of the potential danger explosive in the ledger, a full house of affluent diners were enjoying the posh atmosphere and cuisine of the restaurant beneath The Plaza Hotel, a few blocks south. A tuxedoed trio of piano, bass and drums played tasteful, low-key dinner music.

Aware of nothing but their own pleasure on that summer night, few of the privileged patrons noticed a well-dressed man seated alone at the crowded bar. If they had, they might have thought that his heavy, acne-pitted face would have been more at home in Long Island City, and in less expensive clothes. But no one noticed the man, and he drank quietly, speaking to none of his fellow customers at the bar, until the sophisticated trio finished its set.

The drummer put down his brushes, carefully cased his sticks, and the bass man leaned his ungainly instrument against the piano. The piano player softly announced a fifteen-minute break, and the trio strolled down from the stand. The pianist lit a cigarette, the bass player arched his back as if to rest it, and all three wandered casually past the acne-faced man at the bar.

They didn't look at the commonplace-looking man, and left the restaurant in no apparent hurry. Behind them, the solitary man at the bar let his flat eyes follow them out. When they had vanished from his field of vision, he turned again to his drink, a faint smile on his lips under unsmiling eyes.

Upstairs, the three musicians blended into the busy crowd in The Plaza lobby. The bell captain gave them a cursory glance and looked away uninterested, and several bellhops watched them enviously as men who had an easy life. The desk clerk didn't even notice them as they walked past the registration desk toward a door marked "Private." The door opened as they neared it, and an elderly woman came out carrying a small, blue case.

She bumped into the musicians. "Oh!"

"Easy, Ma'am," the drummer said, steadying the lady.

The blue case fell to the carpeted floor. The piano player bent quickly to retrieve and return it to the lady.

"Oh," she said again. "Thank you, young man."

"Our fault, Ma'am," the piano player smiled.

The elderly woman smiled in return, and walked off on shaky legs. The three musicians waited calmly until she was out of sight, then turned again to the door marked "Private."

Inside the hotel security office, a middle-aged hotel security officer sat yawning behind a high counter. Busy with paper work, he bent in concentration over the counter. To his rear, the heavy vault stood open, its rows of personal security boxes shining in the office light. Intent on his laborious filling of forms, he failed to hear the faint click of his door opening.

The door closed softly.

There was a step.

The security officer glanced up, his middle-aged face breaking into the required pleasant smile accorded all hotel clients.

His smile was never completed.

A macabre figure in a white stocking mask rushed toward the security man.

"What . . . !" the security man began, half rising on his stool.

He saw a blurred, white glove, a heavy, automatic pistol coming down toward his head, and nothing more as the pistol slammed against his skull, leaving only the pain and a roaring silence.

Breathing hard, the white-masked figure bent over the security man where he lay crumpled on the floor behind the counter. Straightening, he gave a low whistle, and two more white-masked men entered the security office. Like a well-trained military assault team, the three went to work swiftly.

The man with the gun grabbed the ring of keys from the belt of the unconscious security officer. Another followed him into the vault. The third stationed himself at the door, a second gun ready in his hand.

With practiced speed and silence, no single wasted motion, the two men in the vault went down the rows of security boxes, dumping their contents into a large, airlines bag as they went, and placing each emptied security box quietly on the floor each time. Every box was emptied, most containing very little, but each item of obvious value. The two men took no time to examine anything, simply opening and dumping, opening and dumping, until they had finished—the boxes all empty, the bag almost full.

The man with the gun zipped the bag shut, turned, and left the vault. Without a word, the second man followed him. They stepped over the silent security man. The third man opened the door, looked out, and nodded. All three men stripped off their masks and gloves, slipped them into special pockets inside their tuxedo jackets, and the three musicians stepped out.

Closing the private door gently behind them, the trio ambled back the way they had come. In the lobby full of travelers, no one remarked about the unobtrusive airlines bag carried by the piano man. The three strolled across the lobby, and went down into the restaurant once more.

They climbed back onto the bandstand, the drummer leaning down to talk to a gushing, overenthusiastic drunk, while the piano player placed the airlines bag casually into the bass man's instrument case. With a cool nod to the waiting diners, the pianist took his seat at the keyboard, and the other two musicians set themselves in readiness.

"Number four," the piano player said. "One . . . two . . . three . . ."

The scream rolled through the lobby of The Plaza some ten minutes later. A middle-aged woman, dressed for traveling, came out of the security office in a daze. As the desk clerk and bell captain ran up, she tried to speak, but nothing came out. She pointed shakily to the open door of the security office.

At the door, the desk clerk gaped at the shambles— the rows of empty deposit boxes piled neatly on the vault floor. He looked around as if sure someone would explain it to him, make it all go away. The bell captain, after a single glance, hurried into the room and bent over the fallen security officer.

"Out cold, but he's breathing," the bell captain said to the desk clerk without looking at him. "You better tell Mr. Deroux fast, and find Harry Dalton."

"What? Yes, of course," the desk clerk said, but he didn't move, as though paralyzed.

A brisk, bantam rooster of a little man pushed through the gathering crowd of onlookers and into the office.

"What's going on here? Let me through!" he commanded testily. "Security chief! Let me through. What . . . !"

He reached the desk clerk, and stood there gaping at the mess, the fallen guard, and the kneeling bell captain. He and the clerk looked like astonished Doublemint twins—neither seemed able to move or speak.

"Maybe ten minutes ago, Harry," the calm bell captain said, looking up at the security chief. "They didn't leave a postage stamp."

"They?" the security chief, Dalton, said.

"Had to be more than one, a fast job," the bell captain said.

"I . . . I've been in the lobby an hour," the security chief stammered. "I didn't see anyone, hear anything. Nothing at all. How could . . . ?"

The bell captain said, "Isn't anyone going to tell Mr. Deroux and get the doctor down here?"

Blinking, the desk clerk moved at last, turned in a daze, and walked to the desk to call the manager and the doctor.

"No one," the security chief said. "The whole lobby. Over an hour. I didn't see anyone at all!"

The scream in the lobby had echoed faint and distant down in the plush restaurant where the trio oozed its low-key sounds. None of the jaded diners, wrapped in their comfortable cocoons of personal pleasure, heard the scream. The acne-faced man at the bar did hear it, and so did the piano player. Unseen by anyone else, the piano man looked toward the man with the acne scars, and allowed a barely discernable grin to play across his cool face. His fingers made a light, quick run on the keys.

At the bar, the acne-scarred man finished his drink, stood up without any sign at all, and left the restaurant.

Up in the security office where the doctor was now working on the reviving security officer, the manager of the hotel stood beside his security chief looking grim.

"No one," the security chief said again. "I didn't see anyone. I was looking right at . . ."

"You'll be looking for a job if we don't get it all back, Dalton," the manager said. "Have you thought of maybe calling the police?"

"Police?"

"It's customary," the manager said scathingly. "Damn it, Dalton, call the police!"

Red-faced, the security chief hurried toward the desk. But all the way he was still muttering to himself.

"No one. I didn't see anyone. How . . . ?"

7

The sun of another clear, warm morning shone low through the high windows of the gymnasium on an upper floor of The Waldorf-Astoria. Alone in the vast space, Charlie Chan was silently engaged in a series of strange, fluid, ballet-like calisthenics. Deep in total concentration, Chan was unaware of the entrance of Jimmy into the gym.

The dapper, younger detective, his clothes not quite so neat now and his eyes tired, stopped to watch his father. The grace and suppleness of Chan's movements, despite his age and weight, made Jimmy stand for some minutes with unconcealed admiration. But when Chan finally completed his exercises and sank slowly to the floor into a lotus position, Jimmy hid his open approval behind a careless smile as he approached his father.

"So you're still at it, Pop?" Jimmy said, grinning. "The old T'ai-Chi-Chuan—gives pliability of child, health of lumberjack, peace of mind of sage!"

"Ancestors may not be all wrong," Chan said dryly.

"Me, I'll take *karate*," Jimmy said, slashing with his hand at the air. "Hah—yah—ho!"

Chan smiled. "Number Three son traitor to ancient heritage. Favor upstart Japanese, feeble imitators of great Chinese original."

"I guess maybe you're right, Pop."

"Sometimes am," Chan said. He picked up a towel, started toward the showers. "You have news?"

"We've questioned them all now," Jimmy said, following Chan into the shower room. "The servants look okay, but not much else does."

Chan undressed, and stepped into the shower. "Details, please."

"Well," Jimmy said, taking a seat on a bench while Chan went to work scrubbing himself under the hot water, "the servants admit they were all running around cleaning up after the party, no one was around the foyer after the guests left. They also say there were deliveries all day yesterday, and the whole staff was busy as hell. Seems Cosmo was a demanding boss, they were all scared of him, so they ran around doing their jobs, and didn't keep much watch on deliverymen. They admit someone could have snuck in pretty easy."

"Problem of harsh ruler," Chan said from under the running water. "Dog afraid of losing job if make mistake, often fail to see tiger approach if not instructed to watch for tiger."

"Yeh. But they're clean, I figure. They were paid pretty high, more than usual, so they liked their jobs. None of them was left any money in Cosmo's will. They're pretty glum about looking for new jobs."

"Who was left dead man's fortune?"

"No one," Jimmy said, "and Cosmo wasn't that rich, it turns out. He lived high, kept up a big front. What he did have goes to his charities. No one gets a cent, not even that Natalie. Even the house goes to a museum."

"No surprise," Chan said. "Victor Cosmo large ego, leave cash to build immortal name, not help living people."

"Funny, but that Natalie didn't seem surprised, either," Jimmy said. "About getting nothing, I mean."

"Some women appear without brains, but know their man," Chan said, grunting as he switched to cold water. "Have heard alibis of four guests from party?"

"Every comma," Jimmy said wearily. "Lorraine McCall was with her agent yesterday morning, had a long lunch with a producer—he confirms it. But she was alone, napping in her apartment, for three hours before the party. Her maid was out the whole time."

"So, no alibi," Chan said through teeth clenched against the frigid water. "She was where after the party?"

"Straight home, she says. Says maid was asleep, she sat up a while thinking about her past. Something reminded her that maybe the past hadn't been so bad."

"Indiscreet early film mentioned by Cosmo," Chan said, groping out for his towel. "Can believe her. Mistakes of youth and fire can taste sweet in the mouth of advancing age."

Jimmy shrugged, still too young to understand. "Winston Cleaver was with his 'boy' all day yesterday, he says. Took the guy shopping to make up for leaving him to go to Cosmo's party. The 'boy' confirms it, says he squeezed two suits and a bikini swim suit out of Cleaver—for what his word's worth. Even so, Cleaver had an hour alone before the party, and afterward he went to a gay bar to feel better. He was there, but no one's sure when. It's a tough, hoodlum-run dive. Bad contacts."

Chan stood drying himself. "Jeffrey Lowman?"

"The 'candidate' won't say where he was yesterday before 3:00 P.M. At three o'clock he was in a meeting at City Hall, that's sure, but he left by five, and was alone a couple of hours. After the party he drove around alone, planning how to finance his campaign without Cosmo, he says. His chauffeur backs him, but the chauffeur's been with him almost ten years."

Chan put his exercise suit back on. "Innocent rarely have alibis, life full of unobserved hours. Strong alibi sometimes point unerringly at killer."

"Then we're out of luck all down the line," Jimmy said, following Chan out of the gym toward the elevators. "That weird artist character, Lalique, was at a gallery until after lunch yesterday. Then he went home and did yoga for three hours! No one around, of course. After the party, guess what he says he did, Pop?"

"Imagination of simple detective not equal to such a task," Chan said. "Tell, please, hour too early for small games."

They left the elevator, and walked to Chan's suite. Jimmy closed the door, and trailed Chan into the bedroom where he sat down grinning while Charlie opened a closet to select a suit. Chan chose a dark suit this time, held it as he looked at his grinning son.

"Suspense is killing," he said dryly.

"Lalique took a swim, Pop—in Central Park Lake! That's what he says. He said, 'To dare is necessary.' Only he says no one saw him, not even a cop. I got the feeling he was hoping to get arrested, make the papers."

"Am sure he was," Chan said. "Lalique great painter with printer's ink and name in columns."

Jimmy nodded, but his face wasn't happy. "That's it then, Pop. No alibis, before or after, but no proof, either."

"Proof, in case such as this, come on change of wind," Chan said, adjusting a black tie before his mirror. "What of most important ledger?"

"Not a trace of it in the house or in Cosmo's office. His lawyer says he never heard of it. But . . ." Jimmy hesitated, and watched Chan. "Something kind of peculiar *did* happen last night. It could be nothing, a coincidence, but maybe not."

"Perhaps some robbery attempt with connection to Victor Cosmo?" Chan said softly, turning to face his son now.

"How in . . . ?" Jimmy exploded, then shook his head admiringly. "Okay, you guessed it, Pop. Only it wasn't an attempt, it was a real, solid robbery with a clean getaway." Jimmy explained the details of the robbery of The Plaza Hotel's security office. "The crooks got everything down to the last diamond, plus a lot of junk. They didn't stop to pick and choose. And one of those safe deposit boxes belonged to Victor Cosmo."

"Ah?" Chan said, and his veiled eyes were bright.

"Cosmo's lawyer doesn't know what was in the box."

Chan nodded. "You are seeking thieves?"

"Norbitz is running them down. Seems there was a three-piece combo playing the restaurant, and they quit this morning."

"Musicians like mailman, seen but not remembered."

"Something like that," Jimmy agreed.

"Robbery sound as professional as murder," Chan said. "Is urgent to locate thieves, may be more involved than appear."

"We'll try hard, Pop. Where are you going?"

Chan looked down at his unaccustomed dark suit for summer wear. "Must pay respects to shadow of late host. Last act of man sometimes cast light on earlier scenes."

8

The ornate chapel stood on a rise above the glistening Hudson River. In the park at the river's edge, people strolled in the warm sun, the younger couples swinging their arms hand-in-hand. Along the parapet there were even a few stubborn fishermen clinging to the impossible optimism that fish could still live in the once great river.

In the almost deserted parking lot of the chapel above, Charlie Chan stood and looked down on the innocent scenes of life going on. There was a soft sadness on his pale, ivory face, but a firm optimism, too—the same kind of optimism that made the fishermen keep on trying. The great river of the world still had room for life, too. The thought of a forgotten Chinese sage seemed to square Chan's shoulders, and he turned and entered the spacious chapel.

A white-haired clergyman was already well into an impassioned eulogy for the late Victor Cosmo. Against his will, Chan recalled Norbitz's comment when he learned there was to be a formal funeral—"Christ, if they want to bury all of him, they'll have to put the whole bathroom in the box!" They had not put the whole bathroom in the ornate coffin on a bier in front of the intoning minister, but they had closed the lid in consideration of how the philanthropist had died.

Norbitz was uncouth, Chan admitted mentally, yet there was something very human about the blunt policeman, clean and direct. A sense of real life, perhaps better than all the conventional hypocrisy that people used to deal with death.

42

". . . it is always a tragic occasion when a dear one is taken from us," the minister's mellifluous voice droned on. "Victor Cosmo was a man who loved people, and people in return loved him . . ."

Chan ceased to listen as the minister's hollow words echoed through the vast chapel. It was almost deserted, few coming to mourn Victor Cosmo. The servants were there, perhaps not only because the remains in the coffin were those of a man who had paid them well. A few scattered strangers, the lawyer, Chan guessed, and some business associates who kept looking at their watches—and the five guests from the ill-fated dinner party.

". . . yes, dear friends, Victor Cosmo was a man who loved others, and who helped the less fortunate. He gave of . . ."

Chan observed Natalie sitting alone in the front pew. The curvaceous blonde was dressed in black—a chic, designer black, even now, but that, by now, was the only way she could know to dress. Her face was hidden by a black veil, and her slim shoulders moved as she seemed to be weeping. Even at the solemn moment, a few of the younger businessmen were watching her, aspiring to Victor Cosmo's place, but Natalie looked only up at the soothing clergyman.

". . . How do you judge a man's life? By his wealth? No, my friends. By his position in this mundane world? No, again. You judge a man by the work he has done. We see his efforts, and we thank him . . ."

Two rows behind Natalie, alone in the row as were most of the others, Lorraine McCall sat aristocratically erect, a deep sadness on her patrician face. But it was a shallow sadness, Chan saw, like some lady of the manor at the funeral of some unremembered tenant on one of her forgotten farms. An actress, Lorraine McCall could hide her true feelings from anyone except Charlie Chan. Narrow-eyed, Chan watched her fingers idly picking lint from her trim black dress.

". . . We judge him by seeing all the lives he has touched in his passage through this mortal realm . . ."

Jeffrey Lowman sat on the far side of the empty chapel from Lorraine McCall. The politician's face was like a marble statue, perhaps the pose for the statue of himself he expected grateful citizens to erect someday. Lowman showed neither hate nor love, neither sadness nor satisfaction. His was a public face, calculated to reveal nothing and offend nobody. The sharp eyes behind the wire-rimmed glasses were focused straight ahead on some neutral point—wrapped totally in himself, as if no one else were there, not even the coffin.

" . . . and we judge him by the love of all those dear to him whom he has so sadly left behind . . . "

In the exact center of the precisely center row, with nothing but space around him, Lalique sat regally against the pew. He was dressed completely in bright yellow—from shoes to a ribbon hanging from a single earring—with two large, painted black circles on his cheeks! The gaudy painter looked lazily around at everything except the minister, adjusted his yellow-tinted monocle from time to time, and stifled a yawn!

" . . . and so, wrenchingly, we say good-bye to Victor Cosmo. We gently lay him and his great work to rest."

Winston Cleaver, as far back as it was possible to sit in the echoing chapel, pursed his fleshy lips as the minister ended the long eulogy, and muttered half aloud.

"Good night, sweet prince." He reached into his jacket, took out a silver flask, drank once, tapped the cap back on with a gesture of finality, and added, "and bon voyage!"

With a swelling of soft organ music from unseen hands the clergyman, head bowed and hands folded, came down from the pulpit and disappeared as the few mourners rose and filed out. At the door, Chan nodded gently to each of his fellow guests as they passed.

Lorraine McCall paled visibly as she saw the detective, but raised her chin quickly and went on past him. Lalique preened under Chan's gaze, twirled his monocle, laughed, and went on toward his car. Jeffrey Lowman did not appear to notice Chan at all. Winston Cleaver stopped, and held out his flask.

"A farewell potion, Mr. Chan? For Victor—wherever he's gone?" the sinister, teddy bear of a man said.

"Regret must decline generous offer," Chan said.

"A matter of duty, Chan? On a case and all that?"

"Alas, matter of stomach," Chan said.

"Bad luck," Cleaver said, taking a long drink. "You know, if there is a devil, I feel a little sorry for him with Victor about to arrive in his domain."

Laughing at his own macabre joke, Cleaver strolled on across the parking lot to where a handsome young man sat at the wheel of the writer's car. Chan stood for a few seconds staring after each of them. A soft voice spoke behind him.

"Mr. Chan?"

He turned. The blonde Natalie stood there, her veil up to show her beautiful face. Her eyes were red with crying.

"Mr. Chan," she said again, her voice intense, "I want you to catch whoever did . . . this to Victor! Catch him, Mr. Chan, and punish him!"

"Have every intention of doing same," Chan said mildly.

Natalie became silent. She made no move to leave the entrance to the chapel, as if something held her to the last vestige of Victor Cosmo. She looked away across the all but empty parking lot toward the wide, deep river.

"You know, Mr. Chan, I never really loved Victor —until today," she said. "I was poor, a nobody from a dead town a long way from here. A one-movie-house town, with two storefront bars where the farmers got stoned on Friday nights. Victor was my chance, nothing more. He was rich, had contacts, knew how to make me into a model. He came across, I came across, you know? Only, now I think I loved him after all."

"Many never know what have until lose it," Chan said.

"Yes," she said. "That part of Victor you saw the other night at the party, the part of him that was cruel and arrogant, it wasn't the Victor I knew. Oh, it was part of him, maybe there's a bad part of all of us, but he was much more than that. The good part of him was what most people knew."

"Model's mask seems to hide woman of depth," Chan said.

"Oh, I'm pretty dumb, I guess. No schooling, and they expect models to be all face and clothes dummy." She looked at Chan. "You may not believe this, but I guess I was very happy with Victor. I had nothing, and he gave me everything. All I ever wanted, except some slim prince charming. And maybe I had a real prince, if not so slim. Now he's gone. Now I've got nothing again."

"Know of will leaving all to charity," Chan said, "but is possible he left you some insurance?"

"No," Natalie said, "nothing like that. Victor didn't believe in insurance. He thought it was morbid. I expect, too, he never thought of me being without him. He hated any thought of death."

"Not unusual weakness."

Natalie shook her head. "It looks terribly frightening now, the future, I mean. Sometimes I don't understand the world. Why do things like this have to happen, Mr. Chan?"

"Sometimes," Chan said, consoling, "we are all like man who looks up at sky from bottom of well—view of distant clouds very small."

The beautiful blonde gave a faint shrug, smiled, and walked toward where Victor Cosmo's chauffeur waited at the dead man's black limousine. Chan watched her pause for a second to look at the elegant car, as if she were thinking that she would not have such a car to ride in for very long.

For the rest of the afternoon, Charlie Chan reexamined the house and grounds of the dead man. He then paid a quiet visit to the security office of The Plaza Hotel. He found nothing, and, tired and momentarily gloomy, he returned to his suite in The Waldorf-Astoria.

A call to Jimmy brought only the information that Jimmy was out, they did not know where. Sighing and musing, Chan considered his singing nightingales, looked at his watch, and realized that he was hungry.

Undressing, he stepped into the bathroom. Humming softly to himself, the prospect of a shower making the detective feel better after his fruitless day, he laid out a fresh towel, and selected a new cake of his own soap.

Out in the living room the telephone rang. Chan hurried out and picked up the receiver.

"Jimmy?"

"I'm sorry, Mr. Chan, it's the desk clerk. I thought I saw you come in. You didn't come to the desk."

"Excellent suite too inviting a prospect to stop. There is a message for me?"

"Yes. A friend of yours, Mr. Eric Ponce of Honolulu, called earlier. He was unhappy at finding you out, and asked that we be sure to leave the message that he had called. It was in your box. When I realized that you had . . ."

"Yes, so sorry, thank you. Call of Mr. Ponce noted."

Showing a rare irritation, Chan hung up, and returned to the bathroom and his anticipated shower. He reached to slide open the shower door—and stopped. His dark eyes narrowed. He stood there looking at the shower stall, his pale, ivory face pensive. Softly, he spoke aloud to himself.

"*Ponce?* Most common name, man from Hawaii sure to know one such. No *Eric* is friend of Chan, unless old memory fail."

He considered the frosted glass door of the shower.

"Would friend in distant city call without leaving number where he could be reached by return phone?"

Nodding to himself, Chan returned to the living room, got a chair, and brought it into the bathroom alongside the shower stall. Gingerly, he climbed up onto the chair, and peered down over the top of the stall.

"Ahhh," he breathed. "So? Message of *Mr. Ponce* placed in box, inform watcher where annoying detective resides without risk of exposing one who wants information. Professional."

Down where the glass door would open, taped solidly with the pin removed and the arming handle set to release when the door slid far enough, was the twin of the hand grenade that had killed Victor Cosmo.

9

The man with the acne-scarred face sat on a bench in the narrow park between Riverside Drive and the broad Hudson River. A sky of high, purple clouds settled a fading twilight over the city and New Jersey across the river. The man sat quietly in the darkening dusk, feeding pigeons unshelled peanuts from a brown paper bag.

He wore a light raincoat that was buttoned despite the lingering warmth of the summer evening, and sat stiffly tall. He cracked the peanut shells meticulously, removed every trace of shard from the nuts with care, and tossed them to the pigeons, one at a time. Expressionless, the scarred man watched the birds fight each other for each tiny nut.

One dark bird seemed slightly injured, fluttering too slowly to secure a nut. The man began to toss the peanuts so that the injured bird rushed frantically back and forth, missing the nuts by a hair each time.

The man laughed.

At last it was dark in the city, and the acne-faced man's bag of peanuts was empty. He tossed the crumpled bag behind him onto the grass, got up, and walked across Riverside Drive. He moved without haste up the deserted block of Eighty-Fifth Street, just off the Drive. He passed a sleazy rooming house, one of the hundreds of rabbit-warrens on the Upper West Side that rented single rooms with cooking, and asked no questions.

Inside the shabby firetrap, through the open double doors, a paunchy man in a dirty undershirt read a racing form behind a high, battered counter in front of a row of empty mail slots.

The acne-scarred man passed the open doorway without even glancing inside, and seemed to vanish somewhere in the alley beside the flophouse.

In a second-floor room of the Eighty-Fifth Street fleabag, the three "musicians" who had recently soothed the privileged diners of The Hotel Plaza restaurant were lying around in easy relaxation. The piano player and leader was draped in a shabby armchair with his feet up and a cool drink in his hand.

The drummer hunched in another armchair, deeply engrossed in slowly spelling out the words in the paperback confessions of a Seattle housewife who had left her husband and four children for the "free," exhilarating life of a high-class call girl. The drummer frowned heavily.

"Hey, man," the drummer said to no one in particular, "you ever run into a hooker was real happy? I mean, like one ain't layin' it all out for some pimp daddy, hustlin' for leavin's?"

"They're all dead from the neck up," the piano man said, lazily. "White-slaving. They got no life in 'em."

"Yeh," the drummer said. Then he grinned thickly, forgetting his own doubts, wanting to believe the happy, "free" Seattle housewife. "Her old man couldn't give her what they got to have, right? Me, I'd give her. Keep her real busy."

"Sure you would, Jo-Jo," the piano man said. "After the payoff, let's go to Seattle and look her up."

The drummer's dull eyes shone with the prospect, then he began to chew on his lower lip, revealing the inner doubt no one in the world knew ate at him except himself—no one was ever going to know. The piano man only watched him and smiled.

The bass man saw none of this, heard none of it. He was lying on a battered studio bed, staring at the loot laid out on another studio bed. The entire haul from The Plaza was spread out on the second bed in a jumble of jewels, cash and stock certificates. The bass man's eyes gleamed as brightly over the haul of valuables as did the drummer's over his dreams of the Seattle house-wife whose husband hadn't been able to keep her happy at home.

When the knock came on their door, all three jumped a foot. They froze for a moment, then relaxed, their faces revealing that they had been expecting a knock. The piano man drew his pistol anyway as he stood up.

"Sit tight," he said to the others, "no one knows we're here except him."

"Hey, man," the drummer said, "on our way, right?"

"Seattle next stop," the piano man said, and laughed.

Gun in hand, the piano man stepped to the door, opened it cautiously out of any line of fire, and peered out. He smiled in recognition, let the door swing all the way open, and started to step back.

The blast of the shotgun turned the piano man's step into hurling flight—backwards, as he catapulted away from the open door and through the room in a grotesque flailing of limp arms and legs that ended sprawled like a rag doll on the room floor.

The drummer clawed at the gun tucked inside his pants.

Prone on the bed, the bass man never made it up. A second blast from the shotgun ripped a gaping hole in his chest and in the studio bed at the same time, and he lay as if pinned to the bloody bed like a red blot.

The drummer got his gun halfway up, before it was blasted out of his hand and through the window in a shower of glass by a third shot of the shotgun, the hand that had held it dead before the gun hit the concrete in the alley below.

Three shots, three dead men.

Preceded by the heavy, squat barrel of a sawed-off pump shotgun, the man with the acne-scarred face stepped into the blasted room and closed the door. He considered his work for a few seconds, found it satisfactory, and cradled the sawed-off shotgun in the crook of one arm. With his free hand he began to pick among the spread-out loot on the second studio bed.

He searched meticulously at first, humming to himself. Then he began to scowl, and rummaged angrily through the piled-up loot. In a few moments, his black-gloved hand was ripping furiously at the valuables, flinging jewels aside, knocking stock certificates to the floor. No longer humming, he searched the haul like a maddened wild animal.

He got down on his knees and peered under the beds, under every piece of sleazy furniture in the room.

On his feet once more, he tore open all drawers, ripped into the few contents of the single closet, emptied out the three suitcases he found. At last, breathing hard, he stood stock still in the center of the room. Whatever he had come for, killed the three men for, wasn't there.

He looked at the three dead men with venomous hatred—they had tricked him, fooled him! The stupid bastards! They were cheats and liars—unfair! No, not liars, just bums! He kicked the dead piano man.

"Lousy small-timers!" he snarled to the silent room.

Incompetent, that's what the three "musicians" had been, just plain no good at their work. Making him go to all the trouble of killing them without having what he wanted. Bums!

The acne-scarred man vented his anger and disgust with the idiots who had failed him by scattering the gleaming loot across the dirty floor of the cheap room.

He let his rage shake him for a few seconds more, then he took a deep breath, shrugged, and turned to leave the bloody shambles he had made. As he stepped over the sprawled drummer, the dead man came to feeble life. Not quite dead yet, the drummer, with dreams of what he would do to the Seattle housewife, clutched at the faint shadow that passed.

Clinging like a man in a dark sea to whatever passed in the haze of life left before his eyes, the drummer's hand caught the leg of the acne-scarred man in a final death grip—hand holding to one tiny twig that would keep him from slipping down that long, awful last slide into bottomless blackness.

The man with the acne-scarred face looked down without a trace of alarm, almost with interest, displaying the detachment of a scientist looking at some experimental animal that was not behaving precisely as the data indicated. He pumped his sawed-off shotgun, aimed it at the dying drummer, but didn't shoot. He waited like the scientist, timing the final reactions of the laboratory animal. One second . . . two . . .

The drummer lost his grip and, with a faint rattle in his dreaming throat, slid down the chute into death.

The hand fell away from the acne-scarred man's leg.

With a nod of approval and confirmation of what he had expected to happen, the man with the acne scars kicked the dead drummer out of his way. He slipped the shotgun under his raincoat and buttoned it. Holding the gun close to his side under the coat, he left the room, humming.

In Charlie Chan's Waldorf suite, the men of the NYPD bomb squad were working carefully in the bathroom. Chan sat in the living room, dressed once more in one of his white summer suits, watching with interest as the bomb experts worked. He was unperturbed, smiling lightly at his son Jimmy as if simply pleased at having acted wisely enough to save his own life.

Jimmy looked pale. He was waiting with Chan and Norbitz for the bomb squad to finish. The younger detective seemed jittery. Norbitz was calmly eating Cracker Jacks from a box with its top ripped off.

"That stuff'll make your teeth fall out," Jimmy snapped.

"Yeah," Norbitz said, still eating the sugary popcorn, "but you get a prize."

Chan said, "Number Three son is policeman, has seen danger close before."

"You could have been killed," Jimmy said.

"Man who choose to climb mountain as trade, aware of long fall if slip," Chan said.

"Sure, but this guy's a pro, Pop. I don't want . . ."

"Happily," Chan smiled, "even professional makes error of being too clever. Desire to locate Chan's room without risk of suspicion by asking, backfire. Desk clerk remains unalarmed, but Chan not so. Curious performance of alleged 'friend' alert long-wary detective to possible sinister purpose of message. Killer wish to see from safe distance which box message placed in. Possibility cause to look before leap into shower."

"Lucky," Norbitz said, crunching another Cracker Jack. "Well, we know one thing—you make someone real nervous."

"Most true," Chan said, "and nervous tiger often leave wide trail."

"I'll buy that," Norbitz agreed.

The leader of the bomb squad came out of the bathroom. He was carrying the hand grenade, made safe now with a new safety pin. The bomb man tossed it in his hand like an apple.

"No prints on it, of course. Surface's too rough," he said. "Neat job, they sure keep us jumping with what they think of next. No way of tracing it, I'm afraid."

Jimmy said, "Get it out of here."

When the bomb squad had gone, Chan stood and patted his son on the shoulder. The two men looked at each other with wordless understanding.

"You have questioned hotel employees?" Chan asked.

"Yeh, no one saw anyone around this suite," Jimmy said. "Pop, you're on vacation. Why not let me and Norbitz . . ."

The ringing of the telephone stopped Jimmy from finishing his suggestion. Norbitz picked up the receiver. As he listened, he put the Cracker Jack box on a table, and nodded quickly.

"Yeh, okay," he said, and hung up. He looked at Jimmy and Chan. "That was the squad room. They just took a report on a homicide. Three guys gunned down in a West Side flophouse. Shotgun. The descriptions of the dead guys sound just like the three musicians from The Plaza robbery!"

"Ah?" Chan said. "Perhaps trail of tiger is growing wider, may soon be easier to read."

"Pop . . . ?" Jimmy began.

Chan shook his head. "Mountain climber must not look down as summit nears. Come."

Reluctantly, Jimmy followed his father out of the suite. Norbitz left his Cracker Jacks on the table.

10

The odor of smokeless powder hung thick in the flophouse room. Drying blood had spread wide around all three bodies. One was sprawled grotesquely on his back, some ten feet in a direct line from the door, an automatic pistol still not far from his dead hand. Another lay flat on a studio couch as if pinned to it, and the third was on his face with his right fist still clenched, a paperback book lying in blood near him.

"Killer was expected," Chan said, studying the scene, "and was most probably known to victims. Door was opened, and man with shotgun fired before speaking. Little time for two men inside room to resist."

"They were the thieves at The Plaza, alright," Jimmy said.

The jewels and other valuables scattered all over the room told their mute story.

"I know them," Norbitz said. "Heist men for hire from outta town. They wouldn't work for just anybody, you'd have to have good connections to get to them. I guess they shoulda stayed out of town."

"Well," Jimmy said, "you know what Thomas Wolfe said."

"What?" Norbitz said.

" 'You can't go home again.' "

"Smart guy," Norbitz said. "What Wolfe was that? Bookie used to work the Taft was named Wolfe. Augie Wolfe."

"See what they have on them," Jimmy said in disgust.

"You know, Lieutenant, reading can make your ass fall off," Norbitz grinned.

Without waiting for a rejoinder from Jimmy, Norbitz bent over the fallen men. He began to search them, not at all bothered by their mangled condition.

Jimmy and Chan nosed around the cheap room. Jimmy looked in the drawers and closet, noting the evidence of a violent search. Chan observed the scattered loot, got down and peered beneath all the beds and other furniture. Norbitz finished his search of the dead men's clothing.

"Not even a swizzle stick," Norbitz said, rising. "They knew their trade too good to carry anything that could drop and identify them. Too bad for them they didn't know enough to keep a door closed."

"Nothing in the room I can see," Jimmy agreed.

Chan stood pensive, staring down at the scattered loot.

"Unknown assailant kills three men," he said slowly. "Was clearly expected in room where valuables are waiting, possibly for disposal, yet does not take any of jewels or negotiable stock certificates. Instead, makes wild search among items of great value for something else."

"He knew what he wanted," Norbitz said, and glanced at Jimmy. "Sidney Kingsley, that one I liked."

"Would be curious," Chan went on, "except know that safety box owned by Victor Cosmo among those emptied in Plaza theft. Clearly, dead men think valuables are goal of robbery, but am sure there was other motive for crime not revealed to victims."

"You mean the ledger, Pop?" Jimmy said.

"Most assuredly. Perhaps killer hire heist men to secure ledger of late Victor Cosmo, or perhaps someone else. But is certain that killer came here seeking small ledger more valuable than jewels."

"Worth three more murders?" Jimmy said.

"To someone, worth murders without end," Chan said.

Norbitz stood at the broken window, looking out. He leaned, and peered down into the dark alley below.

"Hey, there's a gun down there!"

Jimmy looked out beside Norbitz. "Let's take a look."

The two New York detectives hurried out of the death room. Chan stood alone after they had gone. He let his slow, dark eyes drift all around the room, then down again at the dead men. He stared for some time at the body that lay on its face with its fist clenched as if hanging onto life.

From below, Jimmy called up. "Nothing but the gun down here, Pop! Serial number filed off, and it wasn't fired. I guess one of them got his gun out—and that was all."

At the window Chan nodded, then returned into the room. When Jimmy and Norbitz returned, they found the portly detective kneeling beside the body with the clenched fist, a small vinyl pouch in his pudgy hand.

"Got something, Pop?" Jimmy asked.

"What is it, Inspector Chan?" Norbitz said.

Instead of answering either of them, Chan opened the vinyl pouch, removed a small sheet of clean white paper, a fine brush, a glassine envelope, and a jeweler's magnifying loupe. Holding these ready, Chan carefully forced the clenched fist open. He held the paper under the hand, and gingerly brushed across the fingers and opened palm, and under the fingernails.

"Hey," Norbitz said. "Science, even."

"Shut up!" Jimmy said.

"Pardon me, *Superintendent!*" Norbitz said.

Chan ignored them. He put the jeweler's loupe into his eye and raised the white paper to his face. He turned the paper in many directions to catch various angles of light. He began to nod, satisfied.

"You see something, Pop?" Jimmy said quickly.

Chan nodded. "Killer, it appears, wore blue trousers, and owns a white cat. Of long-haired variety, Angora perhaps."

He looked up at Jimmy. "Most careful and skilled murderer often overlook the unexpected incident. Man with shotgun fail to kill one victim instantly. As passed near, dying man reach to hold his leg. Remnants of death grip reveal that dead man's hand contain cat hairs, also blue fibers under fingernails. No other evidence of cat in room, and none of victims wear blue clothing. Therefore, blue trousers and cat must belong to the killer."

"Great," Norbitz said. "All we gotta do is arrest every guy in blue pants in the city."

Jimmy said, "There must be ten million cats in the city, Pop, one million of them white."

"In murder investigation, nothing is wasted. Never know where may lead. Slender threads weave hangman's rope."

Rising, Chan transferred the contents of the white sheet of paper into the glassine envelope. He replaced his loupe, brush and paper in his vinyl pouch, then handed the glassine envelope to Jimmy.

"Laboratory will no doubt reveal more information than simple eye of Chan," he said.

"Okay, Pop," Jimmy said, pocketing the glassine envelope. "I guess we're through here. I'll call in the experts and the medical examiner."

As Chan nodded, his veiled eyes fell on the night table beside one of the beds. Something seemed to attract his curiosity. Next to a dirty ashtray, under a half-empty pack of cigarettes, Chan's glance had detected the edge of a matchbook. He picked it up. It was one of the wide, ornate kinds given away by nightclubs and the better restaurants. Chan examined it closely, but it seemed to offer little help. The top part where the name of the club or restaurant would have been was torn off.

"Come on, Pop," Jimmy said, waiting in the doorway.

Chan slipped the matchbook into his pocket, and silently followed his son and Norbitz out. As they filed down the dusty stairs, Chan seemed to be thinking.

"Too bad," Jimmy said. "I guess whoever the killer was, he got the ledger he came after."

"Perhaps," Chan said, "perhaps not. Violence of search hint at frustration. Possible someone reached the three thieves first. Would like to ask some questions of man on entrance desk."

"Okay, I'll go with you," Jimmy said.

"I'll put in the call for the meat-wagon," Norbitz said.

The burly partner went on past the desk and out to the unmarked cruiser. Chan and Jimmy stopped at the seedy desk. The man behind the counter didn't even look up at them, he was still reading his racing form, and drinking beer from a bottle.

11

The paunchy desk man had a face that looked like a dented ashcan. His grimy undershirt and stained trousers belonged in the same ash can. With elaborate concentration, his pig eyes bored into the racing form, he sucked at his beer bottle as if secretly amused by the two dapper detectives waiting to get his attention.

"Must ask some questions, please," Chan said politely.

For answer, the paunchy man slowly turned another page of his racing sheet, belched loudly, and shook his head still without looking up at the detectives.

"Jeez," he said, shaking his head and talking to some unseen audience, "Chinese cops. What'll they come up with next? Eskimo judges?"

Abruptly, he lowered the racing sheet, and scowled at the two detectives. "Look, I awready told the other cops I didn't see nothin', okay? Nothin' at all, check?"

Chan's voice was mild. "There is alternate entrance to establishment?"

"Christ! Are you guys thick or somethin'?" The desk man slammed down his racing form. "See that couch over there in the office? That's where I was sleepin'. I didn't see nuttin'. I didn't hear nuttin'. I don't know nuttin'!"

A roach ran across the counter. The desk man's hairy hand moved with sharp reflex and smacked it flat. He flicked the crushed bug onto the floor, and casually wiped his hand on his undershirt.

"Congratulate most well-adjusted man on sleep of baby," Chan said, unruffled. "Very unusual to sleep so soundly that noise of shotgun firing three times fails to awaken."

"Yeah?" the desk man said, half-defiant and half-wary. "Well, I guess I'm an unusual guy, right?"

"Decidedly," Chan said dryly. "Then you saw no one enter just before shots, or exit after same?"

"Hey, you got it!" the man said sarcastically. "Chinese monkeys, that's me. Hear no evil, see no . . ."

"Man of vast learning," Chan said, his irony lost on the slimy desk man. "Perhaps observed stranger enter fine hostelry some time before murders? Someone who possibly ask for room of dead men? At any time during this day?"

"Yeh, I remember," the desk man said. "Sure. A little guy, wearin' a suit of armor, ridin' a white horse!"

The slimy man went into a loud guffaw, slapped his ham hand on the rickety counter. Chan's nose wrinkled in distaste.

"Thank you, very cooperative," he said.

He nodded to Jimmy, and turned to leave. Jimmy was staring at the desk man. Then he followed Chan toward the doors. Behind them, the desk man snickered.

"Hey," he called after them, "I got some dirty shirts. You guys know a good laundry?"

His braying laughter at his own humor followed Chan and Jimmy out into the dark summer night. Norbitz waited at the unmarked cruiser. Jimmy touched Chan's shoulder.

"You get in, Pop. I forgot something. I'll catch up in a minute."

Chan nodded, and went on. Jimmy turned back into the fleabag. The desk man looked up again, smirking and rolling his pig eyes up to the ceiling, as if he couldn't believe the stupidity of all detectives.

"Hey," Jimmy said, almost humbly. "Could you come out here a minute?"

The paunchy slob shrugged, and strolled out from behind the counter. Quietly, Jimmy removed his glasses, tucked them into his pocket.

"Yeah, what the hell you want this . . . " the desk man began.

"You know the story of the mule and the baseball bat?" Jimmy said seriously.

"Jeez," the man said, "you got me out to . . . ?"

Without effort, Jimmy suddenly seized the paunchy man violently by his undershirt. Twisting the shirt into a knot at the desk man's throat, he slammed him heavily up against a wall, shaking the narrow lobby.

"Hey!" the desk man yelled, thrashing in Jimmy's iron grip. "What the hell ya think you're doin'! Leggo of . . . !"

"I'm getting your attention, slob," Jimmy said calmly, and slapped the man's face with his free hand. "You see me yet, slob? Am I getting through?"

"Leggo! I told ya! I don't know nuttin'!"

Jimmy pulled the struggling man forward with both hands, then slammed him back against the wall again. The man's head hit with a hollow *thwack,* his teeth rattling. Jimmy slammed him again. Jimmy's voice was ominous, his happy-go-lucky manner and studious appearance suddenly a mask of controlled ferocity.

"You pay attention now, 'pig-face,'" Jimmy hissed savagely. "You listen good! Don't tell me again you didn't hear anything. The walls in this dump are so thin you could hear a bird crap on the roof! A pig like you wouldn't miss a roach tiptoeing through the lobby or anywhere else in this trap. Who knows, there might be a quarter in it for you!"

Jimmy slammed the choking, protesting man against the wall once more, banging his head until it sounded like what few brains he had were rattling around in there like a pea in a nutshell.

"Go on," Jimmy said, almost happily, "tell me about your dirty shirts again. The Chinese monkeys. I'm laughing."

He slammed the man again—and the paunchy slob suddenly collapsed in his hands.

"Awright! Awright!" he wailed, "I heard it! Sure, I heard the shotgun blast off. So I locked myself in the office, see? I ain't no hero."

"Wow," Jimmy said. "No kidding? You shock me." He slammed the man against the wall. "Okay, now what did he look like?"

"I never seen him!" the desk man gasped. "I swear—
I never seen him! He musta come in the back way,
'n up the back stairs. I never saw no one come in,
'n when that cannon blasted, I hid good, 'n never saw
him come out! You think I wanted to get blasted, too?"

Jimmy tightened his grip again, as if he would bang
the man against the wall all night. The man cringed.

"What about someone coming in before all this?"

"No one come in!"

"Try again."

"No one I didn't know come in!"

"Who did?"

"Some hookers, they use 3-C."

"Who else?"

"Their fancy man!"

"Keep going."

"A numbers runner, Silk Morgan!"

"Nice guy," Jimmy said.

"The boss come in oncet."

"Did the three up there go out?"

"One guy got a bottle."

"How long was he gone?"

"Ten minutes, no more. They was holed up!"

"Go on."

"That's all."

Jimmy gripped him harder. The man almost
screamed.

"That's all! I swear!"

"I hope you swear good—for your sake," Jimmy
said, his meaning very clear.

As a parting hint, Jimmy shoved the man roughly
back behind the desk counter. The man stumbled, almost fell. Jimmy wiped his hands together with distaste, and turned to leave. The man steadied himself
between the desk and the wall.

"I locked myself in the office!" he shouted after
Jimmy. "What the hell would you of done if you was
me, that shotgun blastin' up there?"

Jimmy didn't look back, but under his breath his
disgust mumbled out, "I'd take a bath."

The man was still wailing his protest as Jimmy went
out into the dark street. He put his glasses on again, ad-

justed them, and his studious demeanor reappeared. His step became light, the happy-go-lucky spring back in his actions.

Chan was waiting with Norbitz beside the unmarked cruiser on the street. Norbitz was grinning with appreciation of his partner, while Chan observed his son quietly.

"Modern police methods achieve any additional results?" Chan said quietly.

"He heard the shots," Jimmy said. "Says he locked himself in the office."

"I believe that," Norbitz said.

"Maintains did not see killer enter?" Chan asked.

"Yeh, there's a back entrance and back stairs," Jimmy said moodily. "Says he didn't see any strangers come in before, either. I think he's telling the truth, Pop. He told me who did come in, and it sounds straight."

"No one suspicious?" Chan said.

"No one he didn't know," Jimmy said. "I know them, too. I figure them to be clean."

"Possible . . ." Chan began.

Before he could complete his thought, two amazing figures came tripping along the dark street. One was a tall, slim Caucasian girl with bright orange hair. The other was a long-legged, equally slim black girl with a bizarre blonde wig. Both wore gaudy, abbreviated hot pants, high vinyl black boots, and garish halters just barely large enough to hold their high, soft breasts.

The Caucasian hooker grinned at Jimmy. "Hi, Jimmy honey."

"Hello, sugar," the black one said silkily.

Jimmy reddened, and scowled. Norbitz frowned. Chan looked askance at his son.

"Friends of Number Three son?" he said.

"Business acquaintances," Jimmy said uncomfortably.

The two prostitutes giggled. The tall Caucasian girl began to walk into the fleabag. The black girl lingered a moment on the dark sidewalk, eyeing Jimmy.

"You got the time, honey, I got the . . . "

"Beat it!" Norbitz snapped.

"Hold it a minute," Jimmy said suddenly, his detective instinct coming to the fore. "You girls operate in that dump? You see anyone around the second floor looking suspicious?"

"Ever'one we see looks suspicious," the black girl laughed.

"He means that shotgunning," the other girl said, at once serious. She shuddered. "We didn't see anything, Jimmy. We heard the shots, you know? So we staid locked in. The shots was real close together, then it was a while before I heard someone leave the back way."

"Yeh," the black girl said. "That killer, he wasn't in *no* hurry. Real cool killer, took his time."

"I guess he knew no one was gonna bother him in this place," the white girl said.

"Okay," Jimmy said. "Thanks, girls."

The Caucasian girl nodded, and went into the shabby building. The black one stood there with a long, slender thigh extended. She tilted her head, looked toward Norbitz from under her long, false eyelashes. Her voice became a high singsong—her working voice.

"Is that the handsome Dee-tective Norbitz over there? Oh, my, I got a feelin' for that . . ."

Norbitz went beet-red. His voice was a bellow. "Go ahead! Move it, Mary Heartline!"

Laughing loudly, the black girl followed her orange-haired partner into the sleazy trap.

The three detectives climbed into the unmarked cruiser. Norbitz took the wheel, and Jimmy turned around to look at Chan in the back seat.

"What do you think, Pop?" Jimmy said. "Some kind of double-cross? Or is there more than one killer?"

"Cannot say as yet," Chan said, thinking. "Possibly both are true. Someone hire three 'musicians' to procure ledger of Victor Cosmo. Assume theft was successful. Perhaps ledger already in hands of eager employer of thieves, and someone else send killer on fruitless mission to steal same."

"That'd mean the killer would probably still be out somewhere looking to hijack the ledger," Jimmy considered.

"Logical analysis," Chan agreed. "Also possible that man who hire thieves also man who hire killer. Double-cross thieves. Then perhaps killer has ledger, perhaps not. One thing sure—person who hire killer most worried, and now may be in water deeper than bargained for."

"A hired killer is a hot potato to handle," Norbitz said over his burly shoulder.

"True words," Chan said. "Ledger now more valuable than ever, and also more deadly. Possession is weapon against all guests at Victor Cosmo's party, but is now also damaging proof of multiple murders!"

"Neat," Norbitz said. "Whoever got it, got to figure if it's worth keeping around for blackmail, or so hot he got to get rid of it fast."

"Interesting problem for unknown employer of killer," Chan said softly.

"Well," Jimmy said, "we've got our own problem— how do we find the guy?"

"Trail widens each minute," Chan said. "Fleeing predator make more and more noise in jungle ahead."

"Unless he holes up and sits tight," Jimmy said.

Chan smiled. "Few pursued murderers have patience to act in best interest."

Norbitz nodded grimly as he started the cruiser and drove off.

12

The next morning, four people gathered in the vast sitting room of Lorraine McCall's town house, not far from the house where Victor Cosmo had died. They were the guests at Cosmo's final party.

The height of luxury in the grande manner, the house was a violent palace of eclectic decoration—oriental rugs mixed with art nouveau; Louis Quatorze antique chairs side-by-side with cubist tables and pop-art paintings. The ceilings of the resplendent sitting room seemed to dwarf Lorraine McCall and her three guests.

Nervous, the gaudy little painter, Lalique, sat in a red womb chair. Dressed in pink, Lalique had obviously chosen the chair as a startling blend of shades of red. His Levantine eyes darted back and forth across the faces of the others as if unsure of where he stood with any of them. His expression was one of suspicious belligerence, more than a little paranoid, considering everyone an enemy.

Jeffrey Lowman was the only one of the four not sitting down. He stood, as he had the night of Victor Cosmo's party, against the mantelpiece, as though he always wanted to be where he could see everyone—where no one could threaten his exposed back. Apparently calm and unflappable as ever, he was the tiger of the group, apart and watchful—ready to act, confident, with the confidence born of the killer instincts that had taken him so far in the jungle of New York politics.

Ever the detached cynic, Winston Cleaver lounged

carelessly in a delicate French occasional chair. The pink teddy bear of a man watched everything with a wry amusement—like a visitor in a bizarre zoo where he found the weird animals very fascinating. His only sign of possible concern for himself was a slow rocking that made the delicate chair creak.

Lorraine McCall listened to the creaking of her valuable antique chair with a pinched, annoyed expression. In her mileau in her own grand house, she sat in the center in a red velvet armchair as if she were some queen holding court with her ministers. It was the actress who had been speaking, the royal leader setting forth the problem to be considered and solved.

". . . so, in any case, I believe we'll all have to agree. Whichever one of us first gets the ledger, or perhaps already has it, will destroy it immediately in the presence of all the others."

She looked around at the faces of her guests as if waiting for the signs of agreement. Instead, there was only an uneasy silence. After a moment, Jeffrey Lowman at the mantelpiece shook his handsome head. He smiled thinly at Lorraine in mock admiration for her salesmanship.

"You're quite something, Lorraine. Good, you're really good. I can see how you persuade people to give you so many money-making movies. You know as well as we do, that whoever finds the ledger first will have the same power over the others that poor Victor thought he had."

The actress bristled, then her eyes watched Lowman speculatively. "Really, Jeffrey? No one else here seems to think that way except you."

"No?" Lowman said, both surprise and disbelief in his smooth voice. He slowly looked around at the other two men. "Well, then, we'll all strike a bargain, yes? Even though one of us is certainly a murderer. We'll ask that murderer to be sporting, to play fair. The same way he—or she—played fair with Victor and those three unfortunates last night!"

"Those unfortunates were three miserable animals who I'm sure richly deserved what happened to them," Lorraine McCall said. "And when you speak of murderers, Jeffrey, you might well be speaking about yourself, isn't that so?"

As if all of them had been waiting to see the first claw, the accusation quivered in the high room. Lalique stared at Lowman like someone entranced by a snake. Winston Cleaver went on rocking in the delicate chair that seemed in danger of sudden collapse. Jeffrey Lowman appraised Lorraine McCall with a careful glance.

"No," Lowman said, as if giving the matter careful consideration, "I hardly think so. Alive, Victor could hardly have revealed my alleged sins without hopelessly incriminating himself. I had nothing to gain by his murder."

Cleaver said, "But a lot to lose, Jeffrey? With Victor dead, that ledger could fall into hands that *could* use the facts against you without self-incrimination. So, while you may not have murdered Victor, you could easily be the one who had those three thieves, ah, eliminated?"

"To get the ledger, of course," Lorraine McCall agreed.

Jeffrey Lowman said nothing for a moment. "You know, Lorraine, when the police come across the most savage and brutal murders, they tell me they usually look for a woman. Men tend to be satisfied with more simple methods. Did you know that, my dear girl?"

Lorraine McCall's eyes flickered like a wolf in a dark forest. Her patrician face showed nothing special, but there was the glint in her eyes that showed Lowman's comment had perhaps scored a hit somewhere inside her.

"Yes," Lowman went on, studying the actress, "you're the most dangerous of us, Lorraine. Because you never really feared Victor, did you? The rest of us were intimidated by the deviousness of the man, what he was capable of. But not you, Lorraine. No, you stood up to our late, unlamented old friend and benefactor."

"I'm not a sheep like you, Jeffrey," Lorraine McCall said.

Winston Cleaver waved a languid hand. "But, then,

Lorraine can't be a suspect. Whoever killed Victor *was* afraid of him, I'd say. That's why the murderer killed him—fear."

There was another silence. Cleaver smiled foxily.

"Of course, I doubt that fear was the only motive—fear of Victor personally, that is. I'd say that the murderer is also the one among us who had the most to lose," Cleaver said.

"And who might that be?" Jeffrey Lowman snapped.

"My vote would have to go to you, Jeffrey," Winston Cleaver said shortly. "The rest of us would surely have lost our reputations if Victor had revealed what he wrote in that ledger, but you . . . ? You, exposed, would probably have risked being put away in some dank prison for a long time. A very long time, indeed, eh?"

Lowman laughed. It was a smirking laugh, full of a knowledge of the world and how it worked.

"I doubt that, Winston," Lowman said. "I doubt that I risk ever seeing the inside of a jail unless I ignore too many parking tickets."

"Perhaps," Cleaver agreed. "I bow to your superior wisdom of the halls of power. But you're a cold-blooded creature, Jeffrey. You're the murdering kind." Cleaver smiled his best teddy-bear smile. "The rest of us are far too soft, far too human for that."

At his mantelpiece, Jeffrey Lowman did not reply. He seemed to accept the charge, almost as if he considered it a compliment. Lorraine McCall recrossed her legs in the red armchair.

"Then it seems to be the three of us against you, Jeffrey," the actress said. "Think about it. Those really aren't your kind of odds, are they?"

Lalique had maintained a determined, if nervous, silence through all the charges and countercharges. Now the swarthy little painter shook his elegant head in the womb chair.

"Count me out, Lorraine!" he said quickly. He waved his arms. "I can't trust any of you. You're all against me! The great are always targets for envy! One of you killed Victor. Or even all of you together! All this is an act to fool Lalique! If I came upon the ledger, purely by chance, there's no reason you wouldn't kill me, too!"

"You have a point," Winston Cleaver agreed. "But, then, it applies to all of us, doesn't it? We're all in the same delicate situation—like four rats trapped in the same dark and quite deadly corner."

"Rats with a great deal to lose," Jeffrey Lowman said, "no matter what you try to deny. Jail may not frighten me as much as loss of fame or money frightens the rest of you."

"Murder isn't what we have to fear," Lorraine McCall said. "It's that the ledger will fall into the hands of one of us who will use it against the others. We have to stand together."

"I wouldn't use it!" Lalique cried.

"Nor I," Jeffrey Lowman said firmly.

"Certainly, *I* wouldn't," Lorraine McCall said.

"And," Winston Cleaver said, "if any of us believes that, we're all fools. But we can't believe it, can we, or trust each other. We're not that big a pack of fools."

Having delivered that summation of the situation, Cleaver got up and strolled to the windows of the towering sitting room. The others had no response. Lorraine McCall showed only relief that Cleaver had left her valuable chair intact.

In the ominous silence of the room, Cleaver stood looking out the high windows. Directly below the windows was a narrow alleyway at the side of Lorraine McCall's house where the garbage cans stood ready for collection. Cleaver's little eyes opened in surprise at what he saw below.

A figure was poking around in the garbage cans. An elegant figure in white, a trifle portly—Charlie Chan. The famous detective was examining the contents of the actress's trash and garbage carefully and methodically. Cleaver, watching, began to smile again.

"There's a curious thing about rats," he said over his shoulder without turning. "Corner four of them in a single trap, and one will very likely turn and devour the others."

Now he did turn, and walked back into the center

of the high sitting room. He seemed to wait for any comment, any answer, to his cynical judgment. There was none, the four former guests of Victor Cosmo's last party totally divided now by the gulf of their suspicion, fear, and, perhaps, greed.

"Then our little conference is all settled, eh?" Cleaver said sardonically. "It's every man for himself!"

13

Charlie Chan left the service alley at the side of Lorraine McCall's town house just in time to see the three men hurry out and depart in different directions. None of them spoke to each other, but Lalique and Cleaver both looked toward Jeffrey Lowman's limousine as it drove away.

When all three had vanished, Chan waited for a full five minutes, but Lorraine McCall did not appear. Unobtrusively, Chan came out of the mouth of the small alley and turned toward Lexington Avenue. He carried a large, brown paper bag with a heavy object in it. At the corner he caught a taxi, and directed the driver to take him downtown to the offices of a matchbook wholesaling jobber.

At the matchbook jobber, Chan asked for the merchandise manager. A big, friendly man with the florid face of someone who sold to nightclubs and restaurants and, to be convivial, had to sample his customers' wares each day, the merchandise manager waved Chan to a seat.

"Small matter," the detective said after introducing himself. "Can identify source of this matchbook, hopefully?"

"Honolulu?" the friendly man said. "Great town. Was there in the war. Sure wish we had accounts that far. What's a detective from there doing in New York? A case?"

"Son is New York detective, am giving humble assistance."

"You don't say? Chip off the old block, right?"

72

"Trust block not wooden material passed on," Chan said. "Hope of help with matchbook?"

The big man studied the matchbook with the cover torn off. "No chance. Some of them use the back cover; I could place it that way. But the classier places just leave it all blank except their name on the front. Without the front cover, all I can tell you it's from our premium manufacturer. Most expensive line."

"Could narrow down to short list?"

The manager shook his head. "In New York, the list would run over three hundred places. All you can be sure of is that it's some plush place, or some gaudy joint trying to look big. Even the color doesn't help—ninety percent of them use black."

"Most popular color," Chan said. "Thank you for time."

Outside again, it was past lunchtime, and Chan felt hungry. He hailed another taxi, and rode uptown to The Walforf. As Chan paid the cab and was about to enter the Lexington Avenue entrance of the hotel, a voice called to him.

"Mr. Chan?"

A black, Lincoln limousine was parked illegally at the curb. It had official city government license plates. A man's head leaned out the rear window.

"Mr. Chan?" Jeffrey Lowman said, "may I speak to you for a moment?"

Chan walked to the big car. "Is conversation to be official matter, or unofficial?"

"For me, Mr. Chan, there isn't any difference between the two. Come, get in."

Chan hesitated, then bowed slightly, and got into the back seat beside the suave politician. Lowman leaned forward toward the chauffeur.

"Just drive around until I tell you to stop," he said.

As the big car glided smoothly away from the curb to blend into the flow of noontime traffic, Lowman pressed a button in the arm rest, and the glass partition rose between the rear and the chauffeur's seat.

"We're completely private now, Mr. Chan. The rear is soundproof," the politician said.

"Most reassuring," Chan said dryly.

A faint irritation crossed Lowman's face. "I value privacy in this snooping age, even though I have nothing to hide."

Chan made no response, and Lowman rode for a few blocks in silence—as if he were regaining his composure. When he finally spoke again, the irritation was gone, and his handsome face was a model of quiet sincerity. He pointed to a hospital the limousine was passing.

"You see that hospital, Mr. Chan?" Lowman said. "I was very much responsible for it being built. There was tremendous opposition from many interests both in and out of city government. The land is immensely valuable, of course, and there were many other demands for the money used to erect it. But this city needed more hospitals, so I worked until I got it accomplished. The city still needs more hospitals, and I'm still needed to get them built."

"Commendable effort," Chan said. "Commendable goal for future."

Lowman seemed to consider the detective's comment, and if he found it lacking, he didn't say anything. Instead, he leaned back as if drained by all his altruistic labors, and closed his eyes.

"A few blocks east and downtown, you'll find a large area of public housing. Uptown in East Harlem, too. Both were almost all my single-handed work. Over on the West Side, I spent four years fighting for a Senior Citizen's Center. It's there now, and I take some pride in it."

"Accomplishment is own reward," Chan said.

There was a muted irony in Chan's voice. Lowman heard it with the trained ear of a man who lived by verbal nuances.

"Alright, yes, I received more reward than pride. I admit that. Victor Cosmo was right in a way. But there are two sides to every coin, and I think Victor showed you only the bad side. I've been presented to you in a bad light. I'd like to set the record straight."

"Straight record is hope of all policemen," Chan said. "But like camel track in Gobi desert, not always easy to find when sand blow."

Lowman frowned as if he wasn't pleased with the whole tenor of the conversation.

"I've taken some things that I suppose weren't legally coming to me. Not very moral acts in some people's eyes, perhaps—people who sit back and do nothing in a tough world, who would never do any good because they never get into the fight. I think I've given back far more than I've taken. I've done good where no one else could have. Politics is the dirtiest business there is. Government in this country doesn't operate like a booster's club. You have to play it the way it's set out, or you don't play long."

"Ancient sage once say road to sun lead through darkest tunnel," Chan said.

Lowman chewed his lip. "What I'm saying, Mr. Chan, is that I'm a man who has done an awful lot of good for an awful lot of people, and . . ."

"Including good for yourself," Chan said.

"Alright, including myself. Why not? Must all men in public position be ascetic hermits?"

"History record few grand viziers dress in rags or live in hovels," Chan said. "Question much too complex for answer by one simple man."

"Very well, Mr. Chan, I'll be blunt," Lowman said. "I need Victor Cosmo's ledger. If it should be found by the wrong people and released to the public, well . . . This city needs me, Mr. Chan, and I intend to go on."

"No man indispensable. Except to self."

"I am!" Lowman snapped. "You're a very clever and competent man, I can see that. Formidably so, I think. If the book should come into your hands, and I think it will, I need your word that you will give it to me first."

Chan shook his head. "Terribly sorry, not possible. Ledger is vital evidence in multiple murder case. I would like to help, Mr. Lowman. In not-perfect world your words have certain truth. But your request cannot be."

"Mr. Chan, politics exist on the barter system—give to get. I'm a politician, a good one. If I get what I need, I'll see that you get what you need. You understand?"

"System understood by my people when West still

lurk in caves," Chan said dryly. "What are you prepared to exchange for ledger?"

"Anything, Mr. Chan. Name it."

Chan seemed to think. "I am afraid too high a price paid already for elusive ledger. Lives of four men. After such a price, there is nothing you could have which is worthy to exchange. Please to stop car."

Jeffrey Lowman watched Chan. His sincere facade was gone now. His eyes were icy, the naked calculation all exposed. He watched Chan like a tiger.

"I'm sorry, Mr. Chan," he said. "I'm sorry I can't depend on you. Deeply sorry."

There was an ominous menace in the handsome politician's voice. Abruptly, he pressed the button that rolled down the glass partition, and snapped at the chauffeur.

"Stop here. Mr. Chan is getting out."

Chan got out, the door closed, and the limousine drove off without Lowman saying anything more. On the sidewalk, Chan watched until the car vanished into the heavy traffic, then he hailed a taxi once more to return to The Waldorf.

14

Sound City Recording Studios were on Manhattan's Upper West Side—an ordinary yellow-brick building like any warehouse. Jimmy Chan got out of his unmarked cruiser, and went into the building.

Inside, the building was unlike any warehouse. The main recording studio was a huge, cavernous room the size of a major gymnasium. The walls and ceilings were constructed of movable wooden slabs that adjusted to whatever acoustical requirements the sound engineers needed at a given moment. At one end was the control room. Separated from the inner studio by a thirty-foot glass partition, the control room looked like the interior of a spaceship.

Jimmy moved through the maze of electronic equipment and controls, dazzled by the endless banks of dials that reminded him of a visit he had once paid to NASA headquarters. He headed for the main control room. As he entered the soundproofed enclosure, an explosion of sound like a bomb came to meet him. It seemed to hammer at him from everywhere, booming out of monstrous speakers suspended high above on the studio walls.

In the control booth, dwarfed by the labyrinth of electronic instruments, a small man sat twisting dials. He was a short, bearded man in clothes as violent as the sounds he was coaxing out of the mixing console. Totally engrossed in his work, the short man swayed and moved his head to the beat of noise as he jiggled his dials and buttons.

The noise from the speakers was a wild cacophony of

77

amplified sounds, deafening but somehow intriguing, as if, no matter how chaotic and random they might have sounded, there was a control, a purpose, like a weird composer making music only he understood. A kind of music—a symphony for a madhouse.

As Jimmy Chan walked toward the short man, a heavy thumping effect became slowly dominant in the noise, overpowering all other sounds. The short man seemed to bounce in a kind of ecstasy at the console, his voice raised as if talking to a vast throng of listeners.

"You all know what that is, man? That's the beat, man, the heaviest beat of *all* beats! The beat of life, boys and girls—the human heart!"

The short man worked his dials, and the thumping receded. It was slowly replaced by a hissing rumble that built and built until it sounded like the spewing of a volcano.

"Dig it! Dig it!" the short man cried aloud. "Gastric distress, friend! A growling belly in thirty-two tracks! The duodenum, man! The juice of life!"

Whirling every dial within reach, the short man leaped about in a frenzy in his console chair. The sounds melted together, rose into a sheer wall of sound of awesome, overpowering, almost frightening intensity.

"The human body!" the short man yelped. He looked upward toward the soundproofed ceiling, toward the heavens. "The sound that He laid down, cats. Life in every roaring decibel!"

With a wide sweep of both hands across the dials, the short man ended the sound. Abruptly, like a gunshot. All sound ceased, leaving only the hammering echo, the lag of memory. An all-pervasive silence filled the control room. The short man lay on his banks of dials as if exhausted.

He raised his head, and looked at Jimmy with soft, Italian eyes. His voice was low.

"Death," he said, "death . . ."

He held the moment for a long beat, like one of his own recordings pausing for dramatic effect. Then he sat up, shut down the master switch on the vast console, and leaned back in his chair with a gregarious smile.

"So, what's shakin', Jimmy?" he said.

"I am," Jimmy said. "You do that often, Dials?"

"Got to test the equipment," Dials Grassi said. "I heard it all, man. Got to keep the juices flowin'. It's my high, I guess, Jimmy. Sound. A bigger dose every day."

"The hi-fi junkie, Dials?"

"Something like that," Grassi agreed. "So? You didn't come here to analyze my psyche, did you?"

Jimmy held up the small reel of recording tape that had been sent to Victor Cosmo the day before his party.

"I need a favor, Dials," the New York detective said. "What can you tell me about this tape? Anything and everything."

Dials Grassi took the tape, cued it up on the console, and flicked switches. The death threat blared out like an explosion.

"Dear—Victor—for—all—of—the—pain—"

Grassi sat hunched in his console chair listening intently to the death message. He played it through twice, the second time with his eyes closed, leaning back in his chair. His face was totally objective, neutral—an expert listening to nothing but a product of electronic wizardry.

"Far out, man," Grassi breathed. "But definitely a downer, man. Yeh, yeh!"

He opened his eyes, then played the tape once more.

"An amateur job. Hear all that hiss, Jimmy? Made on a small, home mono machine, and not by an expert, either. Real cute little job."

"The words were recorded one at a time from the radio," Jimmy said. "Right? Then spliced together?"

"That's how it sounds to me. I think I even recognize a couple of the voices. All-night jocks. I don't sleep so good."

"What else can you give me?" Jimmy asked.

"Conventional tape, buy it anywhere. Home stuff

again. Nothing special needed to record it," Grassi said. He thought. "Lemme try something."

Dials took the tape and put it into a chemical bath. After a moment he removed it, and, before it could dry, sprinkled it with iron oxide powder. Jimmy watched, and saw the flat of the tape begin to show striations like those on a light spectrograph. Dials took something that looked like scotch tape, placed it over the flat recording tape, pressed lightly, and lifted it off. He showed it to Jimmy.

"Well, what is it?" Jimmy said.

"It's a permanent impression of the striations on the tape," Dials said. "Almost as good as a fingerprint, my boy. See that thin stripe running across the length of the tape?"

Jimmy studied the marks of the tape. "Yeh, I see it."

"Means that the machine that made this tape has a nick in the recording head. When the death threat was recorded, the head scratched this stripe in the tape."

"You mean," Jimmy said, "that if I find the machine, you could identify it as the one that made the tape?"

"Right on, dad," Dials nodded.

"It'd stand up in court?"

"Now I don't know about that, probably with expert testimony—like mine," Dials grinned. "What kind of case is it?"

"Homicide," Jimmy said. "Four of them—so far."

Dials whistled. "Heavy, man."

"Heavy enough for someone," Jimmy said grimly.

"So turn the rocks, man. Find the machine, I'll identify it for you."

Jimmy smiled, extended his open palm. Dials Grassi slapped it lightly.

"Later," Jimmy said, turning to leave.

Dials went back to his console. A bizarre sound emanated from all the speakers. It began as a low rumble, and rose in pitch until it seemed to spiral upward toward the sky like an incense of sound. Rising and rising until it suddenly vanished into a soundless vibration so intense it couldn't be heard but only felt. A sound beyond living human ears, like some weird salute to the dead.

"For the victims," Dials Grassi said.

Jimmy left.

15

Satisfied with his lunch at the hotel, Charlie Chan walked east toward the river and the elegant enclave of Beekman Place. At a fine, old brownstone he entered, and walked up to the top floor. He rang the bell.

There was a long silence, although Chan could hear movement inside the apartment. Suddenly the door flung open, and Lalique stood there in a grand pose. Chan blinked.

"Ah! Mr. Chan!" the painter said.

He was dressed now all in white—from head to toe, even to a white monocle! Only his swarthy skin and dark hair made a break in the dazzling whiteness.

"So good to see you again!" Lalique showed teeth as white as his suit. "We must talk, yes? Explore genius!"

"Regret this is not purely social call. Have business on mind. Sorry to disappoint by low level of problem."

"Business?" Lalique's white eyebrows went up. "Oh . . . that business. I see, well . . . well, come in."

Chan followed the strutting little painter into his top floor suite—and stopped. For one of the few times in his career, his dark eyes registered astonishment.

Lalique stood facing Chan with his Cheshire cat smile.

The entire apartment was a complete, staggering, endless white! Not the smallest hint of any color anywhere beyond the dark, Levantine face of the painter, and one tiny black point on a stark white couch that was the nose of a white toy poodle. The walls, ceiling, floor, carpeting, furniture, drapes, and everything else down to the fake potted plants were all the same flat, dazzling, maddening white.

"Remarkable," Chan breathed at last. "You feel it is a time for white."

Lalique was delighted. "Ah, somehow I knew *you* would understand, Mr. Chan! Yes, yes, we are two great minds!"

"Again you flatter simple detective."

"No, I don't think so," Lalique said, turning to look around him. "Yes, this is to be my White Period. White is space, purity, cleanliness. White is an escape to peace and serenity. I must have peace. I must now be enveloped in white. No hint of darkness."

"White also color of innocence," Chan said. "Or possibly need to feel same."

Lalique's dark eyes flashed, but he said nothing. Instead, he moved to a white coffee table where a white pitcher and several white glasses stood on a white tray. The painter poured some liquid into one of the glasses. It was milk. He looked up at Chan inquiringly.

"Refreshment, Mr. Chan?"

"No, thank you."

"It isn't simple milk, of course. No, nectar from your own homeland—coconut milk! Delicious."

"Alas, taste never acquired over many stubborn years. Coconuts look pretty on tree."

"A matter of taste. Perhaps some goat's milk? I have some in my kitchen. Alas, try as I did, I could locate no camel's milk in New York."

"Fortunate shortage," Chan said with relief.

Lalique smiled, and sat down. He waved Chan to a white fur easy chair. Chan selected a straight wooden chair instead, also white. Lalique nursed his glass of coconut milk.

"Please, tell me what you can about Victor Cosmo," Chan said quietly.

"There is nothing to tell, Mr. Chan," Lalique said. "Except that I take considerable satisfaction in knowing that dear Victor is dead and buried."

"It is true, as charged by late host at party, that you do not paint your own paintings?"

"The charge of a plebian," Lalique said, waving it

away. "I am *above* painting my own pictures. I inspire them. Lalique is *living* art! I leave the mundane painting of canvas to the mechanics."

"Still, others may not understand. Expect man who sign name to hang on living-room wall at great expense to have painted pictures with hand not inspiration."

Lalique shook his head. "There is nothing dishonest about Lalique. Many great masterpieces were not painted by the men who signed them, but by mechanics in their studios. The truth is merely what people *believe* to be true, *hein?* If I am recorded as a great artist, then I *am* a great artist. And if a great artist is not recognized, then he is *not* great. It is as if he never even existed."

Chan considered. "Then if one commits murder, but is not apprehended, it is as if the murder had not been committed at all?"

"Exactly," Lalique smiled.

Chan nodded slowly. "Except for awkward presence of dead man. Your theory is most interesting, but possibly does not translate well from field of art to field of murder."

"Ah, perhaps that could be so," Lalique agreed, and his dark face frowned. "Who was Victor Cosmo? A nothing. Less than nothing. Little more than a leech. He had no talents or abilities of his own, and because of that he had to surround himself with those who had one or both. A failed artist in his mind, so he had to live vicariously from true artists. But though he needed them, he also hated them. They reminded him of his own emptiness, so he had to try to destroy them."

"Man about to be destroyed have little love for potential destroyer."

Lalique swore angrily. "Victor was filth! He deserved to die. Yes, any one of Victor's guests would have been glad for an opportunity to end his venom."

"Opportunity obligingly presented self," Chan said. "Tell me, of all guests present last night, which would you most suspect of unusual crime?"

Lalique sipped at his coconut milk as if savoring the juice, pondering the question in all seriousness.

"Lorraine McCall is a talent, has mental strength,

but she is an emotional woman. She could have done poor Victor in on the spur of the moment, but she is not capable of murder with full premeditation."

"Grenade imply definite plan," Chan said.

Lalique seemed not to hear. "Natalie? No, impossible. She has the brain of a flea, and the devotion of a child. Victor's death was an act of intellect, a work of slow hate."

The painter drank and smacked his lips. "Winston Cleaver? Ah, yes, I would suspect him of the required ability. He has a devious mind, a solitary cunning. He is an observer. There is something very strange about that man."

Chan nodded. "Jeffrey Lowman?"

"Oh, yes! I would suspect him of anything. He is totally corrupt, and must hide it. Too, he moves in the mundane world where murder can solve problems, eh? I would believe anything I heard that our Mr. Lowman was accused of doing."

"So," Chan said, "then you would narrow our suspects down to three?"

"Three?"

"Without doubt," Chan said softly. "Winston Cleaver, Jeffrey Lowman—and yourself."

"Ah?" Lalique seemed to breathe.

For a brief, flashing instant, the eyes of the two men made contact across the blinding white of the room. Lalique smiled. He said nothing.

"Of the three," Chan said, "who is now to be most suspected in eyes of Lalique?"

"Why, *myself*, of course," Lalique laughed. "Because, obviously, I am the most ingenious."

The Cheshire cat grin broadened on the swarthy face of the little painter. He pushed his glass of coconut milk away as if giving himself more room, and leaned back where he sat.

"But, then," he said, "you shouldn't believe anything I tell you, should you? You must never believe anything anyone tells you, but especially not me, eh? After all, words are really useless things. Men will lie. And I? I have no belief in words at all. They are toys to be played with as the mood moves one."

"Agreed," Chan said, "but eyes will not lie. Silent eyes reveal more secrets than spoken volume. Eyes, perhaps, that must see color of innocence to relieve bite of guilt."

"And just what do my eyes tell you, Mr. Chan?"

Chan stood up. "You have been most helpful. Thank you."

"That is all?" Lalique said, a faint edge in his voice. "In what way have I been helpful?"

"Will know later," Chan said. He walked through the mass of white to the door. "Probably not help in way intended."

With a final smile as enigmatic as Lalique's own Cheshire cat grin, the detective left the apartment.

For a time, Lalique sat there without moving. He stared at the door where Chan had vanished. At last he pushed the pitcher of coconut milk away from him with a violent gesture of distaste. His Levantine eyes were no longer smiling.

16

Jimmy Chan walked down Broadway in the warm afternoon sun. He was in the Lower Forties, an area that was now in sleazy decline. Two prostitutes watched him warily from a doorway, trying to look like two ladies out shopping in what was a men's store. Jimmy ignored them as he passed.

A half a block further on, Chan's third son came close to a blind Negro with a tin cup and a religious sign around his neck. At the panhandlers's feet there was a large, seeing-eye dog wearing booties and a large bow.

"Keep it clean, Boots," Jimmy said without pausing in his stride.

"Sure, Jimmy," the blind man said, glancing at Jimmy, and then looking straight ahead again with his eyes turned up to the sky.

Jimmy continued on until he reached the alcove entrance to a busy tourist restaurant. Customers hurried in and out, but Jimmy wasn't looking at them. He was looking down, as if at their feet. Through the moving legs, like someone standing in a hole below street level, a pleasant-faced man in his forties nodded to Jimmy. His clothes were old and worn, yet they were neat and clean.

"Hiya, Broadway," Jimmy said, moving among the hurrying suckers until he stood over the pleasant-looking man.

The man, called Broadway, wasn't in a hole; he was seated on a wooden platform supported by four wheels with well-oiled ball bearings. His legs were stumps encased in leather shoes. Built into the movable platform was a small display of plastic combs, shoelaces, pencils and cheap, ball-point pens. None of the items had cost more than a dime, yet the sign on the display announced the bargain price of fifty cents each. An American flag completed the display, with a small sign under it proclaiming: "Buy from a Vet."

"Hey, Jimmy," the legless man said. "How's business these days?"

"Don't ask," Jimmy said wryly. "There's a full moon."

"I know what you mean. I hear the wolves out myself."

Jimmy nodded. "C'mon, Broadway, I'll buy you a drink."

Grasping a wooden block in each hand, Broadway pushed himself along the crowded street beside Jimmy. At the corner, the odd pair entered a seedy juice-and-hot-dog snack bar. Jimmy gave the order to the counter man.

"Two Pina Colada."

The counter man wiped his hands on his dirty apron, then drew the two drinks from a bubbling container on the counter. With one drink in each hand, Jimmy led the way to one of the rarely-used tables in an obscure corner of the snack bar. Out on the sunny afternoon street, the streams of people passed like fish in an aquarium.

"Take a seat," Broadway said. "I already got one. No waitin' for a table for me."

Jimmy sat, and for a time the two men sat there in silence, sipping their fruity drinks. Jimmy seemed to be idly watching the passing throng beyond the windows. Broadway only waited.

"What do you hear about last night?" Jimmy said at last.

"About what last night?" Broadway asked.

"The three heist men on The Plaza job."

"Out of town boys," Broadway said. "Suckers, the three of them. Someone must of had good contacts to reach them, but it was a setup. All the way, top to bottom."

"The shotgun man?"

Broadway shrugged, then shook his head.

"Okay, if you don't have facts, give me some vibrations," Jimmy said. "What's the message on the shotgun?"

"Bad vibes, Jimmy," Broadway said. "People are lookin' over their shoulders, you know? Like they don't know enough, and that scares 'em, right? They can't be sure and feel okay because they ain't next, and yet they got a feeling."

"What feeling?"

Broadway drank, licked his lips uneasily. "There's a guy, a button man, been around a long time. A loner, you know? On no payroll. Works by himself, and digs his work. I mean, he *likes* it. On him word comes in whispers. Plenty of big jobs, clean hits, but no record. Lot of smarts."

"He works with a shotgun?"

"He works all ways," Broadway said, then shook his head. "Nah, me, I don't think it was him hit those three heist guys."

"Why not?" Jimmy said.

"Not his style. Word says he don't mess with the average stuff. He's kind of a real weirdo, likes to hit big shots."

"Big shots?" Jimmy said, suddenly alert.

"Yeh, you know, the tough and the rich," Broadway said. "Like he got the hates or likes the risks, gives him his kicks. Now he'd pull a trick like the one on that East Side rich guy. What was his name?"

"Victor Cosmo?" Jimmy said quickly.

"Yeh," Broadway nodded eagerly. "Now that one was his kind of deal the way I've always heard it."

"Does this button boy have a name, Broadway?"

"Nope. Not that I ever heard. Like I said, Jimmy, he's supposed to have real smarts."

"Any kind of name? A place? Habits?"

"He don't work my side of the street, Jimmy," Broadway said. "It's a big city, even down where I am. He's like not a guy at all, just a reputation."

"Does he maybe own a cat?"

"Christ, how the hell would I know that?" Broadway was silent. "I'll tell you, though, guys like he's supposed to be usually have a pet. I mean, no one lives all alone."

Jimmy nodded moodily, seemed to think about men who made their living killing other men for hire—men who lived alone, and killed men they'd never seen or heard of. Everyone had to have something he could talk to, even if he never got an answer.

"Wish I had somethin' more for you, Jimmy," Broadway said after a moment. There was a kind of sad hope in the legless man's voice, as if he needed something.

"No word on any money passing around for the shotgun or The Plaza jobs?" Jimmy asked.

"None o' that'd come cheap," Broadway said, and then was dejected again. "But I ain't heard about no source."

Jimmy scowled out at the wandering crowd as if he wished they'd all go home and stop causing him so much trouble. Then he seemed to hear the hope and dejection in Broadway's voice. He looked down at the neat man.

"How's it going, Broadway?"

The legless man shrugged, looked away. "Tap city, Jimmy. They got their hands in their pockets."

"Come to think of it, I need some shoelaces," Jimmy said lightly. "Let me have a brown pair, okay?"

Broadway held up the laces, grinning to cover the nervous anxiety in his eyes. Jimmy offered him a bill.

"Gee," Broadway said, eyeing the bill, "I don't have change for a twenty, Jimmy."

"So you'll owe it to me," Jimmy said.

Patting the legless man once on the shoulder, Jimmy rose to leave.

"Jimmy?" Broadway said. "Can you fix a ticket for me?"

Jimmy sighed, shook his head. "Give it to me, you damned con artist."

Broadway smiled, almost shyly. "Thanks, Jimmy."

Jimmy flicked the legless man's face with his hand, a pat of understanding, and left the snack bar. Jimmy was smiling as he went; he liked Broadway. Then he began to frown—he was thinking of the shadowy hit man Broadway had described.

Jimmy scanned all the faces going by. Somewhere, one of the faces in the vast city was a killing machine, a human animal with a piece missing inside him and a cat for company. But where, and how to find him? Him—and the one who had hired him.

17

Charlie Chan left the subway at Eighth Street-Washington Square, and walked west through the small, narrow, pleasant streets of Greenwich Village in the warm afternoon sun. Whenever he visited New York, he always rode the subway at least once to feel closer to the ordinary people of the city, to sense what they were feeling, and the changes in them.

He reflected that while the great city had certainly changed, in a way it had not changed that much. It was dirty and dangerous, but it had always been those things, as was most of the world outside the clean, safe, walled-in suburbs. A matter of degree and direction, and while many of the changes were for the worse, many were for the better.

Still considering these thoughts, he reached the old brownstone house on the tree-lined street where Winston Cleaver lived. The bank of mailboxes showed that Cleaver's apartment was the top floor. In a building such as this, it would be a loft—one of the cheap, spacious lofts longtime residents had turned into fine apartments, and hung onto over many years.

Chan puffed his way up to the top—and stopped. His veiled eyes shrank into steel points. Winston Cleaver's door was open!

Only a crack, but open nevertheless, so Chan stepped forward softly. At the door he listened. He heard no sound inside. Soundlessly, Chan drew his small pistol, and pushed the door open a few inches.

He saw the expected rough partitions erected to divide the loft into rooms. He saw the old, comfortable furniture. And he saw nothing else. He slipped inside.

The room was a large living room, and it was empty.

Two doors led off the living room. One went into a bedroom where an unmade bed was clearly visible through the open doorway. The other door was closed. Chan listened again—there was sound behind the closed door, a faint movement.

Pistol ready, Chan glided on light feet to the closed door. He turned the knob very slowly, without sound, and slowly let the door open a crack. His dark eyes peered in. The room was an office, a writer's working study.

Winston Cleaver sat before a typewriter, staring in deep concentration. As Chan watched, he saw the fleshy writer reach out and pick something from a table beside him.

It was a hand grenade!

Chan's dark eyes glinted.

Winston Cleaver held the wicked-looking weapon for a moment, then suddenly flicked the arming handle.

Chan flinched involuntarily, all his muscles tensed to fling himself down and away from the door!

The hand grenade burst into a clear, blue-yellow flame, and Cleaver raised it to a cigar he had produced with his other hand. The fat writer lit his cigar with the "hand grenade," and sat back with a pleasurable sigh. He seemed to look at the lighter for a second, then laughed softly.

Chan cleared his throat and entered the study.

"Apologies, but door was open," Chan said.

Cleaver, who was casually dressed in a tan jump suit, looked more like a stuffed teddy bear than ever.

"My friends can be careless, and I've been working," Cleaver said. "My friends will be the death of me yet—but that's the way men who have my, ah, tastes, usually die. 'Most men kill the thing they love' Wilde said, but he was wrong. Most men, including the great Oscar himself, have the thing they love kill *them*, eh?"

"Sad, but too often true," Chan said. "You are better writer than many wish to believe."

"Oh, every hack, like every actor no matter how bad, has one or two good moments. It's like prize-fighters, Mr. Chan. The very worst professional is worlds apart from an amateur."

"You have interesting cigar lighter," Chan said.

Cleaver looked at the hand grenade still in his hand, and laughed aloud. "Yes, I bought it only yesterday —a small souvenir of dear Victor. I think I'll have it engraved with the date of his untimely demise."

"Am sure Mr. Cosmo would appreciate sentiment," Chan said. "You think Victor Cosmo killed by thing he love?"

"Probably. The problem is to know just what it was that Victor loved—if anything," Cleaver said. He put the grenade lighter down on the table. "I assume you're here to question me more, Mr. Chan?"

"Disagreeable part of my vocation."

"Ah, yes, your vocation," Cleaver said amiably. "To hunt, question, badger, stalk mercilessly. Do you have the ferret instinct, Inspector? But, of course, you must, eh? The thrill of pleasure when you've cornered some unfortunate, driven him to final despair?"

"Keep always in mind last screams of murderer's victim," Chan said dryly. "Mr. Cleaver, you are writer of clever mystery novels. You are most familiar with methods of murder."

"Familiar? Why, Mr. Chan, I'm a *scholar* on the subject," Cleaver said. "A veritable expert."

"Men who acquire special knowledge, have tendency to sometime make use of same."

"Of course. I've put it to use many times. Of course I killed Victor Cosmo!"

"So?" Chan said, watching the fat man.

"I killed Victor in fourteen novels. He was my inspiration. Victor was that sort, you see. Why, without my friend Victor, I don't think I'd have enjoyed writing so many novels in which I murdered the same victim over and over."

"Common belief that most writers portray own experiences, only thinly disguised."

"Please, Inspector," Cleaver said, looking pained. "Give me a little credit. In my last book, I dispatched one of my victims with the skin secretions of a Colombian Kokoi frog. It is a poison four thousand times more potent than cyanide, and all but undetectable. Now would a man with a flair and knowledge like that resort to splattering his victim all over the victim's own bathroom? Ugh, very crude."

"Point is of some small merit, but exotic weapons more easily obtained in fiction than in real life," Chan said. "Also, in your own books, Mr. Cleaver, central character is very often shown to be unpredictable."

Winston Cleaver shook his head, then hunched toward Charlie Chan.

"My books, Mr. Chan, serve a useful social purpose beyond simple entertainment. They are a harmless outlet. I give my readers what they need—brutality, sex and murder. They read about it, live vicariously in my pages, and so have no need to engage in the real thing. That includes myself. My murder of Victor was done on paper; I had no more need to do it in reality."

"Perhaps," Chan said. "Yet, like the others, you hated Victor Cosmo—and not on paper. Am not sure paper murder would truly satisfy."

Winston Cleaver ignored the last of Chan's words, or did not hear them. His fleshy, pink face took on a distant expression, as if seeing something far from his study that only he could see.

"Hated him?" Cleaver said. "No, it was far more complex than that. You see, at one time Victor and I were the closest of friends. True friends, not like the others. He could be a kind, generous, warm and always charming friend. But all of that depended on you remaining dependent on him, the *weaker* of the two in the relationship. If you rebelled, dared be independent of him, then his fascination with you wore off. And when that happened, Victor changed."

The flabby writer drew on his cigar, and studied the pure white ash. "Like some jungle animal, when Victor changed in his relation to you, he turned on you. That was his flaw. He could not have an *equal* relationship, he was too small for that. Victor's life was tragic, Mr. Chan, because he wanted to be a great man, had the necessary intelligence and drive to be great, but never could be great because inside he was too small a person."

"You have thought much and long about Victor Cosmo," Chan said quietly.

"Yes, I have," Cleaver agreed. Then, abruptly, he turned to his typewriter. "Now, if you'll excuse me, I have chapter three to write in my new novel."

"The subject is again murder?"

"What else?" Cleaver said, his back to Chan.

Chan turned to leave. At the study door he nodded a polite good-bye to Cleaver.

"Pleasant day, Mr. Chan," Cleaver said.

The flabby writer bent over his machine, giving the comic effect of a small bear about to type. Chan left the study. At the desk, Winston Cleaver listened and heard the outer door close. Instantly, he abandoned his work and picked up the telephone receiver. He dialed hurriedly. Agitated, he drummed on the desk as he waited for his connection.

"Cleaver, yes," he said sharply. "He was here; Chan. Yes, he just left. Don't worry, he didn't get anything from me. Let him snoop all he wants to, he won't . . ."

Cleaver stopped in mid-sentence. He turned. Charlie Chan stood again in the doorway to the study behind Winston Cleaver. A small smile played across the enigmatic face of the portly Chinese detective. Wordlessly, Cleaver hung up the receiver.

"So sorry," Chan said. "Returned for hat."

The detective walked a few paces to a small table hidden by an armchair. His hat rested on the table where he had "forgotten" it. He picked it up with a brief bow to the watching Cleaver, then returned once more to the study doorway. There he paused, and looked back.

"Tiger who has eaten prey, sometimes roar loudest," Chan said. "Pleasant day to *you,* Mr. Cleaver."

Still smiling, but with no humor in his dark, hooded eyes, Charlie Chan left the apartment.

18

Jimmy Chan sat at an umbrella-shaded table in the open-air cafe of Rockefeller Center. The younger detective's Chinese face was tired and drawn. He watched the other patrons of the open cafe moodily. Behind him, and up above on street level, the water of the Prometheus fountain cascaded in the warm summer afternoon.

The bright, animated cafe was like a giant goldfish bowl. Set down below street level on what in winter was an ice-skating rink, the footwalk above was lined with sightseeing tourists who gaped down at the relaxing customers of the cafe. Jimmy Chan was oblivious to both patrons and sightseers, his mind on darker matters. He was not happy with his progress so far on the case.

He was so engrossed in his worried thoughts that he did not see his father come down the stairs. Chan, conspicuous in his white summer suit and panama hat, had almost reached his son's table before the younger man looked up. Jimmy smiled wanly at his father. Chan sat down, laid his panama on the table, and ordered an iced lemonade from the waitress.

"Nothing for me," Jimmy said, looking at Chan. "How did you do, Pop?"

"Investigation like weaving of intricate rug, pattern does not appear at once," Chan said. "Must patiently gather threads in small bundles."

"That's the slow way," Jimmy said a little bitterly. "We don't work that way most of the time here. We buy our rugs in a store ready-made. Only this time the salesmen are all out of stock. Not one of our stoolies seems to know anything."

"Son has not yet found lead to identity of hired killer loose in city?"

"Not a flicker," Jimmy admitted. "I've got the word out all over town, and I've made it hard—we *want* this guy. But so far I can't even get a whisper of a line on the guy. All we can pin down is that every time he comes up out of whatever sewer he lives in, he uses a different pattern. Then he covers his tracks real good."

"Criminals see movies today, read books, know all ways police have of catching them."

"I've got to give him credit," Jimmy agreed. "He's got imagination. A lot of smarts, like Broadway said."

"Criminal never really have 'smarts,'" Chan said. "Only cunning of fox. May change method of operation all ways can imagine, but pattern remain. In end, will always make error that rise out of actions demanded by his own nature."

"I hope you're right, Pop," Jimmy said. "And I hope he makes his mistake before there's no one left alive to pin it all on him."

The waitress returned with Chan's lemonade, and looked curiously at the portly detective in his white suit. Chan bowed his head with a smile, and the girl left. Chan sipped at his lemonade, his dark eyes thoughtful.

"Son will catch professional gunman, that is task police accomplish well," he said. "But gunman is only arrow, and arrow not as dangerous as hand which draws the bow. One of Victor Cosmo's guests at party hire gunman, and that is murderer we must find."

"We've got them all under surveillance," Jimmy said. "So far, all they've done is bore my men to death. If they want that ledger, they're not working hard to find it."

"Perhaps one already has ledger," Chan said. "Or work in own inconspicuous ways."

"You got nothing out of them this morning?"

"Get much, yet . . ."

"Something on your mind, Pop?"

Chan nodded. "Element which does not fit picture

of case, like sixth finger on glove. What benefit to send Victor Cosmo death threat?"

"I don't know, Pop. To scare him into making a bad move, maybe?"

"Could not succeed, so serves no purpose," Chan declared. "Merely alarm Mr. Cosmo, cause him to take precautions—and allow him time to do same. More simple, and much safer, to commit murder without dangerous warning."

"You mean . . .?" Jimmy began.

"Yes—why was tape sent?"

Jimmy shrugged. "Satisfaction, Pop? We're probably dealing with someone missing a few marbles. At least, off his rocker temporarily."

"Possible," Chan said, shaking his head. "But in case of such hate, satisfaction should be less important than safe results."

Jimmy sighed, seeming to agree. He looked away across the rows of umbrella-shaded tables to the upper walk where the tourists leaned on the railing and watched the cafe. His face darkened as he sensed the fishbowl atmosphere of where he and Charlie sat.

"Listen, Pop," he said, serious. "You mentioned Victor Cosmo taking precautions against his killer. There were *two* precautions, right? Two things he hoped would keep him alive by scaring the killer. One was the ledger, and the other was *you.* Your involvement was supposed to keep him safe. Well, Cosmo's dead, and maybe the killer already has the ledger. That leaves only you."

"Obvious conclusion," Chan said dryly. "Have tried once to remove obstacle of humble self."

"And'll try again," Jimmy said, "so be careful, Pop, okay? Real careful."

"For old man, I still move pretty fast," Chan smiled.

"Maybe, Pop. But there's an old *American* proverb —nobody moves faster than a bullet."

"Will keep Occidental wisdom firm in mind."

Jimmy nodded, obviously unconvinced of Chan's awareness of his own danger, and got up.

"I'll keep digging for that button man," he said.

"And I for finger that press button," Chan answered.

The older detective watched his son walk away through the pleasant cafe, and up the stairs to the street and Fifth Avenue. He sipped his lemonade again, and saw Jimmy pass a man leaning on the railing among the other tourists.

For a second, the man seemed to look after Jimmy.

Chan sat alert, staring at the distant man. But the man's glance toward Jimmy had lasted only a second, and once again he was looking down into the crowded cafe.

Chan saw that the man's clothes were ordinary—and not blue. Just under six feet tall and stocky, even at the distance Chan could see that the man's face was badly acne-scarred.

It was an impassive face, oddly expressionless—a face that seemed to see everything, and react to nothing.

Chan waved for the waitress, and paid his bill. He began to walk toward where the acne-scarred man was still leaning on the rail above. As he reached the foot of the stairs, Chan's eyes met those of the acne-scarred man. A brief, flitting glance. They were cold, bottomless eyes.

Chan went up the stairs.

When he reached the top, the man with the acne scars was gone. Chan looked in all directions, but the man had vanished. Frowning, Chan walked on to Fifth Avenue, hailed a taxi on the cross street, and gave Jeffrey Lowman's downtown office address.

He glanced back through the cab window. For a moment, he thought he saw the acne-scarred man again. Standing alone.

But he couldn't be sure.

19

At Jeffrey Lowman's office, the politician was away at a meeting. Chan waited an hour. Lowman failed to return. Chan left a message, and returned to his Waldorf suite. After carefully checking the shower stall, he showered.

Dressed in his silk robe, he fed his nightingales, and talked to them in his soft Cantonese. Then he stood at the high windows of his suite. An orange sun was setting over the Manhattan skyline and New Jersey to the west. Chan began to go over all he had learned in his mind.

The telephone broke his reverie.

"Yes?" he said into the receiver.

"Mr. Chan? This is Jeffrey Lowman. I . . ."

"Ah, would like to speak with you, Mr. Lowman. Is it perhaps convenient for you to come here, and . . ."

Jeffrey Lowman cut him short. Chan heard the urgency in the politician's voice. All its accustomed assurance was gone. It was the voice of a desperate man.

"I'm going to be killed, Mr. Chan!"

"Danger most often averted by calm mind," Chan said firmly. "Please to explain fears?"

"They think I have the ledger! Mr. Chan, I swear . . . !"

"Have reason for thought?"

"No! I swear I don't have it," Jeffrey Lowman's voice said frantically at the far end of the line. "I told them I don't have the ledger, but I know they don't believe me. They'll never believe me, and they're going to kill me!"

"Who are *they?*"

"I . . . wait!" There was a silence at the other end of the line. Then, "I can't talk anymore here. I think someone is . . . Mr. Chan, listen! I want to tell you everything, the whole story. But I have to tell you in person, someplace where we won't be seen or overheard. Meet me tonight. Say at nine o'clock. On . . ."

There was another silence.

"Mr. Lowman?" Chan said. "You are still there?"

Lowman's voice came on. "Yes, I'm still here, but not for long. Meet me at nine on the walkway of the Brooklyn Bridge. Remember, at nine o'clock. I won't wait long!"

"Yes, yes," Chan said quickly. "I will be there," and he said, "Mr. Lowman? One thing. It was you who engineered the robbery of The Plaza Hotel security office, was it not?"

Chan waited. "Mr. Lowman?"

There was only silence, and the low buzzing of the line.

"Mr. Lowman!"

But the line had gone dead.

Slowly, Chan set his receiver down. Behind his dark eyes, his mind worked swiftly. He picked up the receiver again, and dialed Jeffrey Lowman's office.

He let the phone ring for a long time.

"Yes?" A man's voice said.

"Mr. Jeffrey Lowman, please," Chan said.

"Sorry, sir, but no one's here."

"Are certain? No one there, and all is well?"

"Well, sir? Sure is. I'm the watchman. Mr. Lowman just left a few moments ago."

"Ah? You *saw* Mr. Lowman leave?"

"Sure did."

"Alone?"

"Yes, sir."

"Thank you for trouble," Chan said.

He hung up again, thought, and dialed the telephone for a third time. He called Jimmy's office.

"This is Inspector Charlie Chan. I wish to leave one more urgent message for Lieutenant Chan."

Brooklyn Bridge towered in the pleasant summer night above the dark, old streets of Lower Manhattan. Despite the moon and stars and clear night, the narrow streets of this old area of the city were dark, with a strange sense of a long-past time. There could have been fog, the creaking of wooden ships at the quay, the clanging of horse-drawn trolley bells, and the echoing tread of an old-time foot patrolman.

Charlie Chan, leaving his taxi near the approach to the walkway, watched the cab drive away quickly, and felt the sense of a past time. The great bridge, little changed in over a hundred years, was like a preserved antique. Chan, listening, could almost hear all the sounds of the Gay Nineties, and imagine Steve Brodie climbing up the same footwalk he was about to take.

At the midtime hour, neither early nor late, traffic on the bridge roadway below the footwalk was light.

Chan started up and along the walkway of the towering old bridge. Made of wood, the walkway was exactly as it had been when the bridge was first built—a monument then to engineering genius. Chan moved cautiously along the deserted walkway until he reached a set of iron steps that led up to another long level of the walkway. As he reached the top of the steps, he paused.

The entire panorama of New York stretched out before him from the high, old bridge; the tip of Manhattan with a myriad lights still bright in all the tall buildings; the Brooklyn shorefront; the Statue of Liberty far out in the great harbor; the lights of the tiny islands that dotted the Upper Bay.

Chan stood drawn by the magnificence of the sight, by the mute testimony of what man could bring to the world once he learned to control himself. The thought made a full circle, and brought him back to the purpose of his presence on the fine old bridge—what man could do when he did not control himself. He walked forward again on the narrow wooden walkway toward the high center of the bridge and Brooklyn beyond.

He was out over the deep estuary below, misnamed the East River, the lights still blazing like diamond beacons all around on the land, when he saw Jeffrey

Lowman ahead. The shadow of the tall man was some seventy yards ahead, his face clear under a walkway light. Chan smiled across the distance, but it was too far in the night, and Lowman wasn't looking toward him.

The tall politician was standing quietly, looking out over the dark water far below. Even at night, his handsome, reassuring profile was clear under the light, chiseled like some modern god. Lowman seemed to be admiring the clear night, and the city he planned to lead soon.

Chan did not call out; Lowman would not have heard him anyway. The detective continued walking softly, not wishing to seem too urgent and perhaps alarm the politician. Also, if possible, he wanted to delay as long as he could, to give Jimmy a chance to arrive. Lowman had sounded like a man ready to confess, and men can change their minds—especially killers.

Chan unbuttoned his suit jacket so that his pistol was more readily accessible. As he reflected that perhaps he should have changed to a dark suit, he saw a dark car coming along the roadway below from the Brooklyn side. It moved slowly and alone, its bright lights on as if illuminating the scene on the bridge ahead of it. Jimmy? Looking for Chan? The portly detective peered toward the oncoming car, ready to wave and reveal his presence, when the thought struck him—what would Jimmy be doing on the Brooklyn side of the river?

Yet, it was possible, but . . . ? Chan watched the car more closely. It was all but stopped now, some dozen yards beyond Jeffrey Lowman and still behind him. Chan saw that it wasn't a police cruiser, but a nondescript Ford with its license plate mud-spattered, the numbers conveniently obscured.

Chan sensed the danger!

He began to walk more quickly toward the unaware Jeffrey Lowman who was still staring out over the dark water below.

The faint sound of a car window cranked down.

"Mr. Lowman!" Chan cried out. "Mr. Lowman! Run!"

Jeffrey Lowman seemed to blink, his head turning

slowly toward Chan. Frowning, his face puzzled, Lowman turned to look toward Chan with maddening slowness.

"Run!" Chan cried again. "Run, Mr. Lowman!"

Uncomprehending, as if his mind were still somewhere else, his attention still on his long study of the river and the city, Jeffrey Lowman just stood there.

A shotgun barrel appeared at the open window of the old Ford below on the roadway.

"Down!" Chan called. "Down, Mr. Lowman!"

The shotgun fired twice. Two shots in rapid succession, so close they were like a single shot. A pump shotgun.

Jeffrey Lowman, hit by both shots as he turned at last to look straight at the solitary car below, was hurled against the railing of the walkway.

His tall figure broken in half, his chest a sudden mass of blood, Lowman catapulted over the railing to fall like a stone into the river so far below.

Falling, like the silent ghost of Steve Brodie, into the swirling pools of black water beneath the old bridge.

20

Chan was still calling as the shots exploded.

"Mr. Lowman! Down!"

His voice and the shots seemed to hang in the warm night air of the bridge for an endless moment.

Jeffrey Lowman was gone.

Chan stood there in the blinding light of the solitary car's bright beams. He did not look after the vanished politician. If the shots had not killed Lowman, the fall would have. Chan did not waste time or thought on what could not now be helped. The moment was now the present, and for a frozen space of time the moment hung in suspension.

Then Chan moved. He was a portly man, and not young, but he had the training of T'ai-Chi-Chuan and a healthy life. He was no longer accustomed to running —but now he ran.

Chan ran for his life.

He ran back along the walkway toward the Manhattan side. It was the direction from which Jimmy would come—if Jimmy would come in time.

The solitary car came along behind him, moving faster, closing the gap between it and the running detective.

Chan was in condition, but he wasn't fast. He ran with all his strength on the narrow footbridge with the yawning abyss of the river below, but the car came on inexorably.

Ahead, Chan saw his one chance—the immense concrete and brick main bridge tower on the Manhattan side.

He increased his effort.

The car below was almost up to him.

The shotgun blasted once. One of the walkway's old cast iron and wood benches shattered just behind the fleeing detective. The echo of the powerful gun reverberated from the bridge like a howitzer on a battlefield.

Chan ran on, not wasting motion in looking back or down at the menacing car.

The shotgun blasted again.

Barely a yard behind Chan's head, the buckshot skittered and ricocheted through the thick bridge cables, sending a shower of sparks into the dark air like a Fourth of July sparkler.

The massive bridge tower loomed just ahead. Chan dove for its cover. The shotgun exploded a third time —chipping concrete and brick dust from the tower only inches above Chan's head as he reached safety.

Behind the great tower, sprawled on his hands and knees, Chan rested for a second. But only a second. His "safety" was only a thing of the moment. He scrambled up. Behind the protecting tower, he could not be shot—but it was only an island in a sea of danger. He could risk leaving neither way—backward or forward—and the man with the shotgun could come up to the walkway and find him at any second.

Chan listened behind the thick tower.

The car had stopped below.

Chan heard a sound—the sound of a car door opening, and the metallic ring of something like a shotgun barrel striking against a car door.

Chan looked around, his eyes searching for a way out, while his ears listened for the first footsteps to reach the wooden floor of the walkway.

He saw no escape from his safe cul-de-sac. He heard no footsteps yet—but he heard something else.

Another car.

From the Manhattan side, coming the *wrong* way on the Manhattan bound roadway, the car approached with a squeal of burning rubber and groaning metal. Chan peered out toward the Manhattan end of the bridge. He saw the black police cruiser.

The car door of the old Ford slammed closed below, and the car started up. With a grinding of gears, the Ford began to speed straight toward the oncoming police cruiser. Chan stepped out from behind his shelter on the walkway. He saw the scene almost directly below him.

The two cars were hurling headlong toward each other.

Then the police cruiser whipped into a broad slide across the roadway, coming to a shuddering stop almost blocking the whole road. Chan watched Jimmy and Norbitz jump from the cruiser on the side away from the still-speeding Ford. Jimmy gripped his big .357 Magnum. Norbitz, with a police special, jumped into the shelter of the rear fender of the cruiser. Jimmy took the front fender. Without ever taking his eyes from the speeding Ford in the brief seconds as it raced toward him, Jimmy called out.

"Pop! Pop! Where are you?"

"Am safe!" Chan cried. "Attend to business!"

Norbitz was firing.

The old Ford swerved and skidded wildly, slowing sharply in its attempt to dodge the shots.

"Killer is in car!" Chan cried out.

"Where's Lowman?" Jimmy shouted, sighting down his big pistol, holding it in both hands, and firing at the dodging car.

"Dead! Fall to river!" Chan called.

Jimmy's first shot missed, shattering only one of the Ford's headlights.

Jimmy steadied his gun, fired twice more, squeezing off the shots.

This time both shots found their mark, booming through the Ford's windshield until it became a spider web of shattered glass.

Out of control, the Ford skidded, hit the guard rail, almost went over, bounced back, and came to a stop parallel to the railing, its nose facing Manhattan.

A great silence descended on the old bridge.

The Ford still swayed, its headlight smashed and its windshield shattered. Nothing seemed to move inside the dark car. No one got out. Neither Jimmy nor Norbitz could see anything through the shattered wind-shield in the dim bridge light.

From above, Chan looked down. "Jimmy?"

"Get out of here, Pop," Jimmy said. "You can't do anything now. Meet us down at the foot of the bridge. It's you he wants now."

"For once agree with Number Three son," Chan said above the policemen, his calm voice imperturbable.

Chan's footsteps echoed going away.

Norbitz and Jimmy kept their eyes fixed on the now silent Ford, their guns pointed at it.

"I think maybe you got him," Norbitz said.

"Maybe," Jimmy said.

Norbitz reloaded his revolver. Jimmy holstered his big Magnum, and drew the Beretta from its shoulder holster. He snapped back the slide. The two detectives looked at each other.

"How you want to do it?" Norbitz said.

"Right and left," Jimmy said. "Use the shadows just in case, and have an angle on him in case he comes up shooting."

Norbitz nodded. "Let's go."

Cautiously, the two detectives came out from behind the cover of their cruiser. They moved up each side of the dark roadway toward the Ford whose engine was still idling as it stood silent in the roadway.

Nothing moved in the battered car.

The two detectives came closer.

"Watch for that shotgun," Norbitz said.

"You bet . . ."

Jimmy's mouth was still open, talking, when with a roar the idling engine of the Ford erupted.

The car hurtled at the two detectives.

"Jump!" Jimmy cried.

Cursing, Norbitz raised his pistol, but stood his ground.

The Ford swerved a hair—aiming straight at Nor-bitz.

The burly detective got off one wild shot that missed, and dove for the side of the roadway.

Jimmy fired twice as the car roared on past.

It didn't stop, fishtailed around the parked police

cruiser, and roared away toward the exit ramp, leaving a trail of falling glass and metal.

Both Jimmy and Norbitz fired after it.

Then it was out of range and almost off the bridge.

Jimmy and Norbitz raced to their cruiser, jumped in with Jimmy taking the wheel. The younger Chan roared the cruiser into reverse, slewed it around, and was off after the fleeing Ford, still visible just exiting from the bridge into the small streets of Lower Manhattan.

The cruiser raced down the exit ramp in pursuit. A calm figure stood at the curb just at the exit. Chan waved to the two detectives. Jimmy skidded to a screaming stop just long enough for Chan to enter the rear seat, and then was off in violent, grinding pursuit.

21

They raced along the almost-deserted streets of Lower Manhattan.

"There he is!" Norbitz shouted.

The bullet-riddled Ford was several blocks ahead on the dark avenue.

"He's heading uptown for the traffic!" Jimmy muttered.

"I'll get help," Norbitz said.

While the burly partner picked up his radio-mike to call for squad cars to converge and block the Ford ahead, Jimmy put the accelerator to the floor, and the cruiser powered ahead, topping eighty on the city street.

Still two blocks in the lead, the Ford charged on through a red light, sending a startled panel truck careening up onto the sidewalk. Jimmy didn't even pause to look at the white-faced driver of the panel truck.

As the traffic began to grow heavier nearing midtown, he turned on the cruiser siren.

"Hang on, Pop," the younger detective said. "Now it's going to get rough."

The Ford was still in sight, racing on through the thickening traffic despite its single headlight and shattered windshield.

Jimmy pursued grimly.

On a westbound midtown street, a green-and-white patrol car raced west, its siren wailing to clear a path. The call had come from a patrol car on the West Side

—the riddled Ford had been seen heading north on the northbound avenue. Now the patrol car was racing to intercept.

As it reached the avenue, it swooped south into the northbound street to cut the Ford off.

"There!" a patrolman cried.

The Ford was almost on top of them. It made a wild, skidding left turn, sideswiped the patrol car, and screeched in a sliding curve into the westbound cross street.

The sideswiped patrol car, trying to recover and reverse its direction, failed to make its turn, burst through a Con Edison barricade, and came to a steaming stop with its nose in a shallow excavation.

The two patrolmen cursed.

One of them picked up his radio-mike.

"He's heading west on Forty-First Street, we're out!"

Disgusted, the patrolman hooked up his mike and sat back.

"Forty-First," Jimmy said. "He's made a mistake!"

"We'll get him at the library!" Norbitz cried.

Swinging the cruiser, with Chan hanging on for dear life in the back seat, Jimmy plunged into a crosstown street and raced west. As they roared across Madison Avenue, Norbitz shouted.

"There he is, coming north again!"

"Damn! Fooled us!" Jimmy swore, jamming on his brakes, and backing toward Madison Avenue again.

Behind them the Ford swayed past, still going at full speed. Siren wailing, Jimmy took off after it. At the right curb a taxi was parked to discharge a passenger. It's door opened in the path of the fleeing Ford.

With a tearing crash of metal, the Ford hit the opened door, ripped it sailing up the avenue. Inside the taxi, the astonished passenger stared out of the gaping hole where the door had been, and watched Jimmy's cruiser go screaming past with its siren open all the way.

The Ford suddenly swerved west, cut in front of a turning truck, plunged into the cross street, and was gone as Jimmy came to a swearing stop behind the blocking truck.

The radio crackled in the cruiser: "Suspect Ford seen on West Forty-Fifth Street heading west at Broadway. Cars in area blocked by traffic."

Jimmy finally inched around the blocking truck, and put the gas pedal on the floor again. As they crossed Fifth Avenue, the heavy traffic moving toward the theater district brought Jimmy to another swearing stop.

"Suspect," the radio intoned, "seen turning east on West Forty-Fourth Street."

"He's coming back!" Norbitz raged.

Jimmy backed hard into a car behind him, gained a few feet of space, then pulled wildly up onto the sidewalk. Going slow as people scattered on the sidewalk, he sheared off a few canopy supports as Chan watched in obvious pride at his son's ability and daring at the wheel of a car, and broke out across Sixth Avenue.

Amazingly, the block between Sixth and Times Square was clear. Jimmy roared on across Times Square. The Ford was not in sight to the south, the whole block of Forty-Fourth Street jammed even across Broadway.

On Forty-Fifth, still driving west, Jimmy suddenly wheeled the cruiser left as if to plunge directly into the brightly-lit theater buildings—and skidded on two wheels into the narrow length of Shubert Alley. Two cars blocked his exit at the Forty-Fourth Street end of the alley.

The three detectives piled out, and ran to Forty-Fourth Street.

"Hey!" Norbitz shouted.

The riddled Ford could be seen stalled in the midst of the heavy traffic down near Eighth Avenue.

Jimmy, with Norbitz and Chan at the rear, ran through the jammed, honking traffic. Crowds of well-dressed theatergoers filled the sidewalks at the intermissions of various shows. The three detectives fought and pushed their way through, drawing angry glances and violent language. They paid no attention, running up to the Ford with their guns drawn.

"Alas," Chan said, even before they reached the Ford. "Bird has flown."

The door on the driver's side of the Ford was open. Jimmy and Norbitz checked it. The car was empty, no shotgun in sight anywhere inside it.

Abandoning it, they separated and worked quickly up both sides of Forty-Fourth Street, peering into the angry or startled faces of the theatergoers. But there was no way to find one man they had never seen among the throng.

They met at the mouth of Shubert Alley.

"Shit!" Norbitz said.

22

Still cursing violently under his breath, Norbitz went back to the Ford to move the traffic around the abandoned car—and to search for any possible clues the vanished gunman might have left. While Jimmy called in to start the machinery moving to get the car off the busy street, Chan explained all that had happened on the bridge before Jimmy had arrived.

"Damn," Jimmy shook his head. "He's always one jump ahead of us, Pop."

"Lucky for aging Oriental father, while performing amazing imitation of flying hippopotamus on bridge, killer was one jump behind," Chan said wryly. "Son's arrival on scene most timely."

"You think Lowman was going to confess, Pop?" Jimmy said, ignoring Chan's compliment.

"To hiring of three thieves at The Plaza, yes. Mr. Lowman desperately need elusive ledger, only one with real fear of exposure. Also, only one real man of action."

"But not the murderer of Victor Cosmo? The guy who hired this button man we've been chasing?"

"Possible, also. Mr. Lowman very devious man. Play all ends against each other as matter of reflex," Chan said reflectively. "Possible he hire 'button man' to kill Victor Cosmo, hire three thieves to steal ledger, then send 'button man' to remove ledger from thieves. Kind of double-cross that would seem only logic to clever politician."

"Then maybe he tried to double-cross the button man," Jimmy said, "and that was a mistake—bang!"

"Voice on telephone was frightened enough for that to have been situation," Chan agreed. "Man who hire lion to protect temple, sometimes wake up to find no longer owns temple."

"Maybe we better take a look around Lowman's apartment," Jimmy said.

"Same thought occur to ancient father," Chan agreed.

Jimmy called in once more to report the death of Jeffrey Lowman, and have the harbor police start the tedious task of trying to recover the body from the swift currents of the East River and the bay.

"Hell, he's probably halfway to Sandy Hook by now," Jimmy said. "They won't find him for days, in case he had anything on him. By then any clues'll be ten fathoms deep south of Bermuda."

Norbitz came back, still swearing.

"Nothin'. The Ford's a rental. Stripped clean as a tourist in a hotel poker game," the bull-like partner said. He looked at Chan. "Cat hairs on the floor under the steering wheel, though, eh, Pop?"

"As yet only satisfying confirmation that on correct trail," Chan said. "But hairs may yet prove fatal to cat lover."

Norbitz nodded, then glanced around at all the people filing back into the theaters after the intermissions. "You know, he could be standing there watching us right now."

"Yeh," Jimmy said, looking around. "Makes your neck crawl, doesn't it. You feel like you're in a shooting gallery."

"Condition of being policeman," Chan said. "Remedy is to move fast on trail that leads in circle to behind man with gun."

"Okay," Jimmy said. "Let's go, Pop."

The fashionable condominium stood on a quiet East Side street. Jimmy parked the cruiser in front of the elegant building, and he and Chan went inside. Norbitz remained leaning on the car.

The lobby shone with light, care and money—all marble and chrome and glass, with lush, real potted plants. Even a real fountain sparkled discreetly in a thin shimmer of dancing water. The floor was thickly carpeted, creating a soundless and hushed atmosphere that made visitors want to remove their hats.

An elderly, uniformed doorman hurried forward as fast as his age would permit.

"Yes, gentlemen?" he said, both polite and protective, as if he admitted that everyone was human, but few were human enough to be admitted *here*.

Jimmy flashed his badge. "Which apartment is Jeffrey Lowman's?"

"Four-G," the doorman said. "You people sure took your time getting here."

"Ah?" Chan said, alert.

"What do you mean we took out time?" Jimmy snapped.

"You came because of my call, didn't you?" the doorman said testily. "I got a report of noises coming from inside Mr. Lowman's apartment. If you'd come right away, maybe . . ."

Jimmy didn't wait to hear anymore. He jumped back to the door, motioned Norbitz to be alert, then rejoined Chan to move quickly through the elegant lobby and into the elevator.

On the fourth floor, Jimmy and Chan exited warily from the silent elevator. They moved quietly down the plushly carpeted corridor. Jimmy had his Beretta out. They stopped in front of the door marked 4-G. Jimmy was about to reach for his ring of keys, when they both noticed that the door was already slightly ajar.

Chan placed a finger on his lips, nodded to the door. In the apartment the lights were on!

Jimmy nodded silently, motioned for Chan to move behind him. Cautiously, Jimmy pushed the door open. It moved without sound on well-oiled hinges. Jimmy stepped inside, with Chan close behind him.

They stood in a large, rich living room, furnished in expensive masculine taste—a living room that had once been immaculate, but wasn't anymore. It was a wreck —ransacked and torn to pieces as if by an animal searching for food in a time of starvation. All the drawers were pulled out and flung to the thick carpet.

Papers and personal articles littered every corner. All the books from rows of bookshelves had been pulled down and hurled away. The chairs and sofas had been ripped open with a knife.

"Jesus," Jimmy whispered. "If it's a search, it must have been a crazy man. The place looks like some damned fanatic ran amuck."

Chan frowned, and shook his head. He moved close to the inner walls, his ear close to the walls. He listened as Jimmy watched, still looking around in wonder at the wreck of the expensive living room.

Then Jimmy froze.

Even from the middle of the ransacked room, the younger Chan heard the faint hint of movement in another room. Jimmy gripped his Beretta tighter. Both men stood absolutely still, their heads moving slowly like radar towers searching for the exact direction of the tiny sound.

Chan pointed at last to a closed door in the left wall.

Jimmy nodded.

The younger detective approached the closed door like a man stepping through knee-deep water, each foot placed down solidly before the next step was taken. On the plush carpeting he made no sound at all. He was still some ten feet from the closed door when both he and Chan heard another sound. A louder noise this time, clear and distinct inside the room behind the closed door.

A window had been raised, quickly, without any attempt to be quiet this time.

"Quick!" Chan cried.

Jimmy leaped for the closed door, kicked it open, and jumped into the room with his Beretta held pointed in both hands.

The room was a vast, indulgent bedroom—and it was empty.

"The window!" Chan urged.

A window was open in the far wall, the evening breeze blowing in the white curtains. Jimmy ran to the window and peered out. A fire escape on the side of the building led down into a service alley.

"Stop!" Jimmy cried.

Two floors below, a dim figure was scurrying down the fire escape, taking the iron rungs four at a time.

"Norbitz!" Jimmy shouted. "The fire escape! Coming down fast!"

Norbitz ran from the cruiser to the mouth of the dark, narrow service alley. He had his police special out. As he reached the alley, he stopped. No one had come out of the alley. Norbitz looked up and saw Jimmy's head at the fourth floor window.

Jimmy shook his head.

Norbitz nodded grimly. Jimmy couldn't locate whoever had come down the fire escape. But no one had come out of the alley, and the high walls of buildings towered sheer around the alley on three sides.

Unless there was some door out of the alley, the man was still somewhere there in the night.

The man with the shotgun?

Norbitz licked his lips, gripped his pistol, and walked firmly into the dark alley.

He advanced very slowly, examining every inch of the walls on either side, searching for anywhere a man could hide. He saw nowhere, and he saw no doors or windows low enough for a man to climb through and escape.

The burly detective's mouth was bone-dry.

He walked on, his footfalls echoing from the walls around him in the night.

A row of garbage cans loomed up to his left. Norbitz aimed his gun, flattened himself against the left wall to let his eyes search behind the row of cans.

There was nothing and no one behind the cans.

Not even a cat moved in the alley.

Norbitz walked forward, his palm sweaty now as he held his pistol ready.

The rear wall of the alley seemed to move to meet him. A wall as blank as the others—no door, and no low windows. Norbitz blinked. But . . . ? The man had to still be . . .

His eyes fell on a dark space along the side of the right wall in the shadow of the fire escape above. As he looked, there was a sudden noise, and a small figure burst out of the sunken areaway that led to a basement door.

The figure made no attempt to attack. It ran toward the open mouth of the alley and escape.

"Stop!" Norbitz shouted.

The figure tried to run faster, stumbled, tripped over a break in the paving, and fell clawing to its hands and knees.

Norbitz was on the man. As he tried to scramble up, Norbitz delivered a violent kick. The kicked man sprawled out flat on his face.

"Don't move!" Norbitz growled. "Not a finger. I don't wanna have to ruin my shine on your face!"

The fallen man lay still. Norbitz bent and snapped handcuffs on him. Norbitz looked to where Jimmy leaned out.

"Got him," Norbitz said.

"Bring him up," Jimmy called.

23

Charlie Chan held the suite door open as Norbitz hustled in his prisoner.

"Good evening, Mr. Lalique," Chan said.

His narrow wrists sagging under the weight of the handcuffs, Lalique forced a wan, sheepish smile. His swarthy face resembled a child caught with his hand in a cookie jar—a very different Lalique.

"No gun," Norbitz said.

The small man shuddered. "I . . . I . . . guns scare the hell out of me."

Even his voice was different, the suave, continental tone having vanished. Chan studied the painter with narrowed eyes. Lalique was dressed now in simple gray slacks, stained from his fall in the alley, a cheap, dark blue shirt, and a plain, dark windbreaker. He looked like an ordinary working man out for a beer.

"Your proletarian period, Mr. Lalique?" Chan said.

Lalique shrugged, his eyes nervous, like a man caught in a big lie.

"Perhaps we now see *real* Lalique?" Chan said dryly. "Or do you know anymore who is real Lalique?"

The little painter said nothing, his nervous eyes still flitting around at the three detectives and Jeffrey Lowman's wrecked apartment like a prisoner who knows the worst is yet to come.

"So?" Chan said, glancing around Lowman's suite. "Did you find what you were looking for, Mr. Lalique?"

"I didn't do this, Mr. Chan!" Lalique cried.

"Sure," Jimmy said.

"You just run down fire escapes for exercise," Norbitz said. "Play hide-and-seek."

"Like swimming in Central Park Lake," Jimmy said.

"No, no!" Lalique wailed. "I . . . I haven't done anything. I found the apartment like this!"

"Then what were you doing here?" Jimmy snapped. "Waiting for a bus?"

"I came to see Jeffrey Lowman. We are friends, I had some business . . ."

"Unaware Lowman friend of Lalique," Chan said.

"A *business* friend, not personal. I came to see . . ."

Chan shook his head. "Doorman not aware of your presence. Report noise in apartment to police."

"I came in through the service entrance," Lalique explained. "I wanted . . ."

The little painter stopped, and licked his lips. The three detectives looked at him. It was Norbitz who put the silent thought into words:

"What was wrong with the front door?" the burly partner said.

Lalique looked around pleadingly, his nerves shattered. Completely rattled now, he began to stammer.

"Well . . . I . . . I mean . . . well . . ."

Jimmy snorted. "Book him, Norbitz."

"No!" Lalique cried, almost cringing. "No! Don't put me in . . . Alright!" The painter sat down on a ripped armchair, his swarthy face turned down to the floor. "I telephoned Jeffrey several times. When he didn't answer, I knew he wasn't at home, so I came here." He looked up, his Levantine eyes haunted. "I came to look for the ledger. I . . . I would be ruined if it ever came out. The prices for my work . . ." He trailed off into a beaten silence.

Jimmy said, "What made you think that Lowman had the ledger at all?"

"You saw Mr. Lowman with ledger, perhaps?" Chan asked.

Lalique shook his head. "I just guessed, but Jeffrey had to have it. You see, the four of us met to strike a bargain. We would all look for the ledger together, and when we found it we would destroy it in the presence of all of us."

He scowled. "But Jeffrey was the first one to refuse to go along with the plan. I realized then that if anyone had the ledger, it had to be Jeffrey. He's the kind of man who would use the ledger! While we all sat around and talked, Jeffrey Lowman would act, ruin us!"

"So you figured you'd break in here and get it, right?" Norbitz pushed.

"I didn't have to!" Lalique cried. "The door was open when I got here, the apartment already like this! I only got here a few minutes before you did. I'd barely started to look around when I heard you come into the living room. I got very frightened, and went down the fire escape. That's the truth, I swear it! I didn't do anything, and I didn't find anything!"

The three detectives stared at the painter with silent, unbelieving faces. The silence seemed to be worse than anything to Lalique. He chewed at his lips, looked at all of them as if begging for them to say something.

"Your arrival here was most convenient," Chan said at last, his voice quiet with menace.

"Convenient?" Lalique stammered.

"Jeffrey Lowman murdered tonight on ancient walk-way of Brooklyn Bridge," Chan said.

"His killer got away from us—not very far from here," Jimmy said.

"Jeffrey?" Lalique gaped. "Dead?"

"His death is surprise to you?" Chan said. "You did not, perhaps, receive telephone call from one who knew of sudden end of politician?"

"Sure," Norbitz said. "That'd bring you runnin' to find that ledger."

"No, I never . . ." Lalique's voice shook, genuine shock quivering in his voice. "You're sure, Mr. Chan? Jeffrey?"

"Quite sure," Chan said dryly. "Portly detective very nearly second half of double feature. Fortunate that son and partner arrive in nick of time with heavy artillery. Mr. Lowman not so fortunate."

"Jeffrey?" Lalique said again, wonder in his voice. "Then he couldn't . . . I mean, the ledger . . ."

"You have now other thought of location of ledger?" Chan said quickly.

"I . . ." Lalique began.

The painter stopped, looked up at them again. Suddenly, he jumped up, his eyes wary.

"I can't be mixed up in this! Another murder? No, I can't be!"

"You're already mixed in it up to your monocle," Jimmy said.

"But . . ." Lalique began to protest.

"*Did* you find valuable ledger, Mr. Lalique?" Chan said.

"No! How could I? You caught me leaving. What would I have done with it?"

Chan nodded. "Perhaps find something else of interest in murder cases?"

"No," Lalique sighed. "The whole evening has been a complete waste."

"I am sure Jeffrey Lowman would agree," Chan said, his voice sardonic. He watched the painter for a moment, then nodded to Norbitz. "You may remove handcuffs, Norbitz."

Norbitz looked at Jimmy. The younger detective was watching his father. He nodded yes to his partner. Norbitz removed the handcuffs, and slipped them back into his pocket.

"You may leave, Mr. Lalique," Chan said.

Lalique swallowed, smiled weakly at Chan, and then hurried out of the wrecked apartment as if he was afraid someone would change their mind. Norbitz looked sourly after the vanished figure of the little painter.

"Why didn't we book him, Mr. Chan?"

"Search is for murderer, not second-story man," Chan said. "No proof of murder yet clear against Lalique. Sometimes, long rope is shortest chain, give plenty of opportunity for suspect to tangle self while running in many directions."

"Myself, I'd rather use a short hose," Norbitz said. "Give him plenty of opportunity to talk while going nowhere."

"Admit method of unpleasant pressure often effective," Chan acknowledged. "But work best when interrogator is sure he has right man. With wrong man, third degree has tendency to produce confession of fear that only confuse detective and give real culprit time to escape."

"Okay, you got a point," Norbitz agreed reluctantly.

"Have second point," Chan smiled. "If Lalique tell the truth, someone here before him. Suggest we search for evidence of third man."

Nodding, Jimmy and Norbitz began to make their own search of the ransacked apartment. Chan wandered casually around the rich apartment, examining rather than searching. Then he sat down at a desk in a kind of television-room-and-study. He went through each drawer with meticulous care.

After nearly an hour, Jimmy and Norbitz came into the study shaking their heads. They had found nothing. Chan was still seated at the desk, a stack of small papers in his hand. The papers had figures on them, and were neatly clipped together.

"Got something, Pop?" Jimmy asked.

"Perhaps something most helpful," Chan said. He indicated the stack of clipped papers in his hand. "Have bundle of charge receipts. Mr. Lowman orderly man who live on large expense account, keep good records. These indicate activity of entertainment for past month."

Norbitz noted the size of the stack, and whistled.

"A swinger," Norbitz said.

"And an influence buyer," Jimmy said. "What's so helpful about those receipts, Pop?"

"Most interesting fact," Chan said. "Four times in week before murder of Victor Cosmo, Mr. Lowman patronize establishment called The Serpent's Eye. No indication of attendance at same place any previous time in many months, and each time Mr. Lowman appear to drink alone."

"Alone?" Jimmy said, and frowned. "That's kind of funny, Pop. That place isn't where most guys would go alone—unless they wanted a two-bit pickup, and that's a risky business for a politician with a reputation. I figure a guy like Lowman could get better class call girls if he'd wanted, girls who could be counted on to be discreet."

Chan nodded. "Son has knowledge of this place?"

"Sure," Jimmy said. "The Serpant's Eye is a kind of discotheque joint on the Upper East Side. Slick decor, classy front, big dance floor, rock music—a dancing sewer. The clientele is mostly a pretty decadent crowd. You know, Pop, bored money types, some drug contacts, crazy kids away from home who can steal the money."

Norbitz said, "It's also a favorite hangout for underworld characters. They like to think they're doing some social climbing in joints like that."

"Convenient place, then," Chan analyzed, "for man of position to make contact with underworld? Would find persons with 'hotline' to out of town 'heist' men?"

"Yeh, just the place," Norbitz said.

Jimmy nodded agreement. "Probably a good place to contact a button man, too. Especially a loner like our 'cat' man."

"Suggest, then, we also visit exotic establishment," Chan said.

They closed the apartment door, and went down to the unmarked cruiser. The elderly doorman watched them leave as if he would have to mop the floor after their passage. In the cruiser, Norbitz took the wheel, and Jimmy turned to face Chan in the back seat as Norbitz drove away.

"What do you think, Pop?" Jimmy said. "If Jeffrey Lowman was behind it all, hired the heist men and the button man, why go to The Serpent's Eye?"

"Search of apartment raise doubts of guilt of Lowman. Hired killer have no real need for ledger except for client. Sure that Lowman arrange robbery of Plaza," Chan said, "but . . . ?"

"But not the rest of it?" Jimmy said.

"Lowman not a man to confess to four murders," Chan said. "A man who would fight in such a case, have nothing to lose. Not fear death if already in danger of conviction for murders. But if only hire thieves, and someone else hire killer of same thieves, then Lowman would confess to lesser crime to save self."

"So you think someone else is also behind it?" Jimmy said.

Chan nodded grimly. "Think hidden employer of button man still walk free."

24

The giant snake head leered at Chan and Jimmy.

"Stay in the cruiser," Jimmy said to Norbitz, "unless you hear trouble."

Norbitz nodded. "You couldn't drag me into a trap like that except to make an arrest."

Two stories high, the giant snake head flicked a mechanical forked tongue. Under the darting tongue, a satanic-looking doorman held the door open for Chan and Jimmy. Deafening rock music pounded out into the night of the sedate East Side street as they went in.

Through a second door—a serpent's eye—the stairs led down into a vast, subterranean cavern. The club, jammed with men and woman, both in bizarre clothes from expensive stores, was on two levels. On the upper level, where overaged males flashed too much money to buy overpriced drinks for overindulged women, tiny tables were jammed together—to reap a maximum number of inflated dollars from a minimum amount of space.

The lower level was a large dance floor and long bar, where flashing strobe lights played violent colors over the writhing bodies of the dancers. Down there the men were younger and more bizarre, and the women were in various stages of chic undress. Their bodies glistened in the gaudy, revolving light. The scene looked more like a savage mass ritual than a dance. Only two men in dark tuxedos sat quietly at a corner of the bar watching. The owners.

Between the two levels, the floor was made of glass,

so that the drinkers on the upper level could watch the dancers down below—another American spectator sport.

Chan sat at one of the tiny tables on the upper level, his sharp, dark eyes surveying every face in the packed room. A half-naked waitress in a snakeskin bikini and hooded cobra headdress, came to get Chan's order.

"A cup of green tea, please," Chan said.

"Tea?"

"Tea," Chan said, smiling. "Green."

"Green tea," the waitress muttered, rolling her eyes to the dirty ceiling of the upper level, and swished away.

On the dance floor below, Jimmy gyrated with a stunning Chinese girl who seemed to know him. Mingling with the mass of bodies, he seemed to be one of them, but his quick eyes never stopped searching the dance floor and the bar.

"Tea," the waitress said, plunking down the cup in front of Chan on the marble-topped table. "Green."

"Thank you so much," Chan said, dropping a dollar for the single cup, and a second dollar with a faintly sardonic smile for the girl.

Now *she* smiled, and tucked the bill between her breasts.

Chan sighed at the nature of humans, and sipped his green tea. It was amazingly good. One was constantly being surprised by humans, too. He continued to let his eyes observe everything while apparently looking at nothing at all. His pale, ivory face was swept with color from time to time by the circling strobe light, and then plunged into semishadow as the beam passed on, as if he were an inhabitant of the dark side of the moon.

After a time, he noticed the souvenir book of matches on the marble table beside an ashtray. He reached into his pocket, and took out the torn book that had belonged to one of the dead musicians from The Plaza robbery. The two matchbooks were the same. His face registered satisfaction; no clue was ever without some meaning.

Chan sipped his tea, and continued the policeman's slow job of watching and waiting.

It was past 1:00 A.M. when the serpent's eye opened to admit a heavy-faced man in a dark business suit. The man stopped just inside the entrance, unaware of three other newcomers behind him who had to push around him and glared as they went by. Oblivious to any distraction, his eyes searched the faces of the crowd.

The revolving strobe light picked out the acne scars on his stolid face.

He now carried his light raincoat over his right forearm, and his slow glance swept the dance floor below the entrance. He seemed to see nothing that interested him, and turned his attention to the upper level. Other new arrivals had to push past him. He paid no attention—a man who would not be hurried at his work.

The doorman appeared. "Look," he said to the acne-scarred man. "You want to move in, or . . ."

The acne-scarred man looked at the doorman. The doorman saw a pair of cold, flat eyes with something in them that was less than human. The doorman gulped, turned, and went out through the door.

The cold-eyed man returned to his search of the upper level. A faint twitch moved the corner of the man's mouth.

He had seen what he was looking for.

Charlie Chan, sipping his second cup of tea, and watching the crowded upper level, turned his dark eyes toward the entrance. He found himself looking into another pair of eyes—flat eyes, without expression.

For a brief second, the acne-scarred man's eyes and Chan's met across the crowded upper level of the violent club.

Chan's glance flickered imperceptibly down to the other man's trouser legs.

His sharp glance flew up again to the man's face.

Chan had seen the white cat hairs on the man's dark blue trouser legs! Now he remembered the tourist he had seen at the Rockefeller Center outdoor cafe—the man who had glanced at Jimmy, and had vanished when Chan walked toward him.

The scarred man began to move across the upper level.

For a millisecond, Chan and the advancing, acne-faced man each became aware that the other knew him, that they were irrevocably tied together now, and that each knew what he had to do. Each knew what was about to happen.

Calmly as he walked, without any trace of feeling or concern for where he was or the crowd of people around him, the acne-scarred man let his raincoat fall to the floor. He held a small, deadly machine pistol that had been concealed by the raincoat.

Without breaking step or hesitating, the man pressed the trigger of the gun, and the burst of bullets exploded in the gaudy club.

The machine pistol spat its stream of death straight at Charlie Chan.

But Chan wasn't there anymore.

Before the raincoat ever dropped from the advancing man's arm, Chan had moved with uncommon urgency again, as he had run on the bridge earlier.

He had pushed over his small, marble-topped table, and had dropped behind it as the gunman opened fire.

The first shattering burst slammed into the marble top of the tiny table, skittering away in a shower of flying lead and marble chips.

Screams filled the pleasure dome of the exotic club, shrieks of fear and frantic confusion. The affluent patrons stampeded for safety, no longer in search of vicarious thrills. They trampled over each other like cattle as they huddled against the walls, dove behind tables, cringed in any dark corner they could find.

The machine pistol fired again, its muzzle lighting the dim upper level with spurts of flame. The acne-scarred man continued his steady advance, firing as he walked without hurry, his eyes on nothing but the small, marble table where Chan hid, as if they were the only two in the whole club.

Then he stopped—not ten feet from the small table that protected Chan.

There was no way Chan could fire around the tiny

table without being seen before he could get off a single shot.

The acne-scarred man smiled for the first time, a thin and wolfish smile, and began to circle slowly to his left.

Below, on the dance floor, the laughing bodies were now screaming and running as the machine pistol exploded above. In seconds, the dance floor was empty, as deserted as the vast concourse of a railroad station when everyone has fled from the path of an advancing army.

Only one figure still remained in the middle of the empty space.

Jimmy, pushing the Chinese girl away at the first sound of gunfire above, stood alone, his big .357 Magnum in his hand. He took the powerful pistol in both hands, and shouted through the sobbing screams of the terrified revelers.

"HEY!"

Jimmy shouted again, "HEY! POLICE!"

From where he stood on the deserted dance floor, he had a full view of the button man above through the glass ceiling.

The acne-scarred man saw Jimmy below through the glass floor, and swung his machine pistol.

Jimmy fired upward.

The range was all but point-blank. Floor to ceiling, no more than twenty feet. Jimmy didn't miss.

The heavy Magnum bullet slammed through the plate glass.

Above, the machine pistol fired a long, dying burst that climbed upward into the dirty ceiling of the upper level.

The acne-scarred man came down through the shattered glass of the floor-ceiling, plummeting among shards of broken glass and debris, to smash face down on the empty dance floor almost at Jimmy's feet.

Jimmy stood with the big Magnum still held in both his hands. He licked once at his lips. On the upper level, Chan rose from behind his tiny table, and looked down at his son and the man sprawled on the floor. In the serpent's eye's entrance, Norbitz stood with his pistol out, staring down toward Jimmy and the dead man.

"Okay?" Norbitz called out across the now silent, echoing space.

"Okay," Jimmy said, his voice dry and hoarse.

The crowd began to emerge from every corner, buzzing as they came. Norbitz started bawling out the orders for everyone to leave, get out, go!

Chan went down the stairs to stand next to his son. Jimmy moved to the fallen button man, kneeled, and turned him over. His acne-scarred face held a thin sneer even in death. Jimmy reached down to the man's trouser legs, and picked some wisps of white hair from the dark cloth. He held the hairs between his fingers, felt them, then looked up at his father.

"The cat helped catch the rat, eh, Pop?"

"Only thing professional of death loved," Chan said. "In a way, one more man killed by the thing he loved."

"Yeh," Jimmy said, and stood up. "One to go. The man who hired him. We won't find any leads on him."

"No," Chan said. "We must look elsewhere."

25

Despite the late hours of the night before, Chan was up just after dawn. If his two brushes with sudden death had affected the detective, he did not show it as he performed his silent T'ai-Chi-Chuan exercise in The Waldorf gym. His ivory face showed nothing at all, lost in total concentration on his ancient system of physical health.

When he had finished, showered, and dressed, he went down to the hotel restaurant for breakfast. He ate well, hardly appearing to think at all. The dead gunman was lying on a morgue table, that was his son's job. They had found no clues to the acne-scarred man's name, and they probably never would. A walking bomb that had passed through the world alone.

His breakfast over, Chan picked up the paper bag he had carried from Lorraine McCall's service alley some days earlier, and went out to catch a taxi at the Lexington Avenue entrance of the hotel. He rode up-town to the yellow-brick building of Sound City Re-cording Studios.

He went in and gave his name at the reception desk. A few minutes later, Dials Grassi came hurrying out to meet him. They talked for a time, Grassi nodding, and then walked together back to the main control booth.

One hour later, Charlie Chan exited from another taxi at the gaudy snake head entrance to The Serpent's Eye. The giant snake head looked cheap and shoddy in the warm daylight—a huckster's trick, the gimmick of cheap carnival minds who fooled only the empty souls of the gullible.

Chan spoke briefly to the patrolman on duty, showed his Honolulu Police identity card, and was waved inside. He went down the musty stairs, the broken glass floor like a gaping wound above him, and went to the bar where a pale-faced barman was keeping busy polishing glasses that would not be used this night. Chan asked for the owner.

The owner was a big, wary man with the hard face of a man who made his living on the desperate illusions of empty lives. Chan's face was cold and grim as he identified himself, and began to ask questions. The big man sweated.

By noon, Chan was bowing politely at the desk of the late Jeffrey Lowman's secretary. The secretary seemed stunned.

"Most unworthy condolences," Chan said. "A great loss."

The secretary nodded. "He was such a fine man. What's this city going to do now?"

"All will mourn," Chan said, his dark eyes hidden.

"Yes," the girl said. "What . . . what can I do for you, Inspector?"

"Regret, must see Mr. Lowman's private office."

She nodded as if she understood the unpleasant necessities of police work, and led Chan to an impressive mahogany inner door. Chan thanked her, and went inside.

He searched for over an hour, and found nothing he wanted. Frowning, he sat down at the dead politician's massive desk. His eyes fell on a memo pad. Scrawls, like unconscious doodles while talking on the telephone, covered the pad. Most were no more than meaningless patterns, but a few clear words caught Chan's eye.

" . . . arrogant . . . arrogant . . . both of us . . . blind idiots . . . must tell . . . must . . . "

Chan studied the random words, and his eyes began to shine.

It was mid-afternoon when Charlie Chan finished his lunch in his suite. Humming softly to himself, he fed some choice crumbs from his plate to his nightingales. Then he crossed to his high windows, and stood looking out on the great city spread out in the warm sunlight.

He continued to hum quietly, from time to time saying a word aloud in Cantonese. He was still at the windows, lost in thought, when there was a knock at his door.

Chan crossed to the door and opened it. "Yes?"

"Mr. Chan?" a bellhop said, coming into the suite. "A package for you. Please sign here."

Chan signed, tipped the bellhop generously, and closed his door. Chan held the small, flat package for a few seconds. The address was typed: Mr. Charlie Chan, c/o The Waldorf-Astoria Hotel, New York, N.Y.

The return address was: Victor Cosmo, The Gaines Building, 196 East Forty-Ninth Street, New York. It was the address of Victor Cosmo's office.

Quickly, Chan unwrapped the parcel. He held a small, black ledger!

Chan stared at the ledger, then crossed to his telephone. He dialed the operator of the hotel, asked for the number to his son's office. Jimmy's voice came on the line.

"Have obtained elusive ledger," Chan announced sharply. He explained how the ledger had been mailed to him.

"You mean Cosmo mailed it to you? It was in the mail all along?" Jimmy wondered. "Pop, you better bring it . . . "

"Ledger safe with me," Chan interrupted. "Son will please officially inform all suspects that I have the ledger, and soon will have murderer."

"Pop, no! Now you listen to . . . !"

"Old-fashioned detective have own poor methods," Chan said. "Invite all who concerned to Victor Cosmo's town house this night at nine o'clock. At that time, Chan can, perhaps, lay minds at ease by naming murderer!"

Over the violent spluttering of Jimmy's protests, Chan hung up. He sat back in a chair, holding the black ledger, and smiling to himself like a deadly dragon.

26

It was another pleasant summer evening, less than a half hour after dark, when Charlie Chan walked up Fifth Avenue, and turned up the steps of Victor Cosmo's town house once more. He let himself in with a passkey, and turned on the downstairs lights. He passed through the familiar foyer where Natalie had so carelessly left her handbag with the house keys in it, and on into the sitting room where the guests had first gathered on the fatal night.

The clock on the mantel where Jeffrey Lowman had stood, now chimed eight-thirty. Chan had arrived half an hour early. In the silent and deserted sitting room, the detective sat down in a large, comfortable armchair. He sat quietly, without a sign of nerves or tension. His eyes closed, he seemed to be going over some plan in his mind.

Chan sat that way for about ten minutes. Then his eyes snapped open.

Somewhere, far off in the vast and silent house, he heard a sound. He listened intently. It came again, faint like a cat moving in the house, or a light, slow step that . . .

Suddenly, the house went black. The lights snapped off as if covered in an instant by a black curtain. No light anywhere—the master power switch had been pulled!

Like a ghost, Chan rose to his feet. He stood unmoving for a full minute, his alert head cocked and listening in the blackness of the great house. Outside, the traffic of the city passed on the streets and avenues, the footsteps of the passersby echoing sharply.

Chan moved carefully through the unfamiliar sitting room toward the archway and into the entrance foyer. His feet made little sound on the thick carpet, but twice he bumped into objects in the dark, listening each time as the reverberation of the sound faded away.

The eerie house was as quiet as a grave. Chan strained, but heard no hint of sound or movement.

In an unfamiliar house, his greatest safety lay in reaching the front door. But each time he bumped into an unseen object, he alerted whoever was in the house to just where he was.

Thinking, Chan groped carefully for the wall of the sitting room. By moving along the wall, stepping ahead only slowly, he could find the foyer without bumping into anything more.

Pleased with his plan, Chan slid silently along the wall, avoiding sideboards and chairs. He passed the pantry door, saw the outline of the foyer archway ahead, and across it the heavier shadow of the front door. He . . .

The sound was directly behind Chan!

At the pantry door!

A loop of thin, deadly wire dropped over his head and around his neck!

Chan reached up . . . reached behind . . . turned halfway . . . struggled to reach the deadly wire . . .

The pantry door slammed shut, the key turned in the lock on the other side, as the wire tightened around Chan's throat.

The thin steel wire cut into his flesh. His breathing whistled, gasped, as the garotte choked the air from his lungs.

Through the minute space between the locked door and the sash, the wire pulled tighter and tighter and . . .

Chan groped behind him, twisted, but his back was pinned against the pantry door, and he could not reach the taut, cutting, choking wire!

His air cut off, the detective's brain began to swim in thick, dark colors, heavy and light at the same time, unable to think clearly. Life flowed away in a heavy, nauseous stream that roared in his ears and yet seemed to fade toward silence, fading and floating away, sick . . .

His lungs straining for air, Chan gathered his waning strength and drew his pistol. He raised it behind his head, and aimed down to where the thin wire came through the door. He fired to sever the wire. The muzzle flash seared his neck.

The wire held!

Behind the locked door, frantic hands pulled the wire even tauter. Chan's legs buckled, thrashed.

He fired his pistol at the wire behind him again . . .
. . . again . . .
. . . flame burned and wood splintered . . .

The wire parted with a snapping twang like a high, musical note!

Chan fell forward to his knees.

He struggled not to black out, not while the killer was there on the other side of the door, not while danger still lurked behind there . . .

In the kitchen, an outside door slammed shut. Distant feet ran away into silence.

Chan kneeled on the floor of the darkened sitting room, his head down, breathing slowly.

He remained that way for some minutes until his breathing eased, his heart slowed, then he got up slowly. He walked around through the kitchen door to the other side of the locked pantry door. He stared at the door.

In the dark there was a small gleam—the reflection of a distant light on Chan's teeth as he showed a small smile.

The lights were on again in Victor Cosmo's house when Jimmy and Norbitz arrived some ten minutes later with the four surviving guests of the fatal dinner party.

"Another party, Mr. Chan?" Lorraine McCall said,

her regal head held high as she entered the now bright sitting room.

"Small entertainment," Chan responded.

The actress shrugged, her patrician composure un-ruffled as she took her seat in a high-backed wing chair. Lalique, oddly subdued in a simple sport jacket and gray slacks, perched on the edge of a French Pro-vincial chair, his swarthy, Levantine face fixed toward Chan.

Natalie began to sit down in Victor Cosmo's favorite chair. The dazzling blonde, still wearing black, paled, and quickly took a different chair. She didn't speak, nor did Winston Cleaver as he leaned against the man-tel—a fat, macabre imitation of the late, handsome Jeffrey Lowman.

Jimmy saw the red welt on Chan's throat and the livid powder burns on the back of his neck.

"Pop . . . what . . . ?" Jimmy began.

Chan signaled his son to silence. "You are five min-utes late," he said. "Had some trouble with gathering guests?"

"Lalique had to 'wash his hands,' " Jimmy said. "He takes a long time to do it. Fifteen minutes."

Chan nodded. "You met, as arranged, in hotel around corner? All others on time—ten minutes before nine o'clock?"

"No one was on time," Norbitz said. "You'd think they didn't want to show up. Except the painter, he was early."

"But lost in men's room fifteen minutes," Chan said.

"I . . . I felt sick," Lalique stammered.

"Can understand problem," Chan said dryly.

For a long moment Chan looked at each of them, then he reached into his pocket, and drew out the small, black ledger. He placed it gently on a coffee table.

"All will now observe ledger responsible for so many deaths," Chan said quietly. "More deadly than gun."

Winston Cleaver and Lorraine McCall both moved at the same moment toward the small ledger. Chan stopped them with a wave.

"Please," he said sharply, "will have full opportunity

to examine ledger later. At moment, we have more urgent task—to reveal murderer!"

Chan watched them all, and began to slowly pace the large room. Silent, he let them watch him like rabbits watching a python. Suddenly, he turned to Lorraine McCall . . .

27

"Miss McCall," Chan's voice echoed in the bright room, "you have statement to make regarding your involvement in death of Victor Cosmo?"

"What?" the actress said, taken aback. "No! I . . . why would you ask me something like that? I never had any . . . "

"Must contradict lady," Chan snapped. "Because it was you who sent death-threat tape recording!"

As the others turned to stare, Lorraine McCall crossed her fine long legs, and sat back in her wing chair.

"Really?" she said. "You can't prove anything of the sort."

"Beg to differ," Chan said. "That which people throw away sometimes reveal more than what is kept. Some days ago, very interesting object discovered in trash at your residence. Sanitation service fortunately slow, fail to remove discarded tape recorder before Chan arrive."

"So I threw away a tape recorder, what does it prove?" Lorraine McCall said.

"Recorder purchased only few weeks before discarded, and was in perfect working condition when abandoned. Recording made on it by Chan, later analyzed and found to be identical to death-threat tape. Technical proof certain, stand up in any court. Both tapes made on same machine."

Lorraine McCall lit a cigarette, her hands shaking. "Alright, it's true. I made the tape, and sent it to Vic-

143

tor, but that was all! I wanted to wipe the smugness out of Victor Cosmo. I wanted to frighten him as he frightened so many others! That was to be only the first of several tapes—each more gruesome than the others. I wanted to see him cringe!"

She smoked harshly. "But that was all. I had nothing to do with his death. His killer just took advantage of the tape to cover his own tracks."

"Require advance knowledge of tape," Chan observed. "Who but you had such knowledge?"

"I . . ." Lorraine McCall crushed out her half-smoked cigarette. "You can't believe I'm capable of murder!"

"At dinner party you seize knife, give convincing demonstration of murderous intent," Chan said.

"You can't suggest . . . !"

"Suggest nothing. Under law, all are innocent until proven guilty," Chan said. "However, to detective, all are guilty until facts prove innocent. Hazard of trade. More practical." He smiled. "So, accusing finger point to Miss McCall at moment. Actress is capable of performing great real-life drama. However, before actress can work, dramatist must create drama."

Chan turned on Winston Cleaver. "Is that not so, Mr. Cleaver?"

"Mr. Chan, I'm impressed," the sinister, teddy bear of a man said, and laughed aloud, the unsuspected vein of iron in him visible again. "How *did* you guess?"

"In your apartment, when you thought I had left, you made hurried telephone call to accomplice. After I had retrieved my 'forgotten' hat, I went quickly to pay telephone, and called all numbers of guests involved. No one answered—except Miss McCall. Since you had reached party, person you called had to be actress."

Cleaver nodded. "Excellent, Mr. Chan. You're more than clever, your reputation is deserved. Yes, I helped Lorraine with that tape. I, too, wanted to watch Victor squirm."

"Winston!" Lorraine McCall blurted out.

Cleaver waved her off. "It doesn't matter, Lorraine.

It began only as a joke, Mr. Chan. A black joke, I admit, but those are the only really amusing kind. We planned to send ... "

"Winston!" Lorraine McCall raged. "No one else called me at that time that day! He's tricked you!"

Chan and Winston Cleaver stood looking at each other. The detective remained impassive. Cleaver nodded slowly.

"Very good, Inspector. I must remember that I am only an amateur, after all," the fleshy writer said. "The warning is very welcome."

"Admission of complicity in preparation of tape also welcome," Chan said. "Gives one more with knowledge of death threat prior to party."

"Then!" Lalique cried suddenly, "the killer must be one of them! I knew nothing before the party that ... "

"Knew more than wish known—and *before* party," Chan said sharply to the little painter. "Mr. Lalique, your presence in Jeffrey Lowman's apartment shortly after his death was very large coincidence."

"That's all it was! A coincidence!"

"Yet meaning of coincidence not always clear," Chan said. "Like first touch of ice to skin, difficult to tell if object is hot or cold." The detective's dark eyes became narrow. "Mr. Lalique, one does not commit break-in on simple assumption or guess. You did not *suspect* that Jeffrey Lowman had the ledger, you were *certain* he had it. You had very good reason."

"No, I was only guessing that ... "

Chan shook his head. "This morning, I converse with owner of club called The Serpent's Eye. After suitable pressure, owner admit to seeing well-known Jeffrey Lowman in contact with piano-player thief who later led robbery at The Plaza. Owner also admit to seeing Lalique in club at same moment. Lalique is not a man who can be missed. Owner convinced that most noticeable artist also observe Jeffrey Lowman and thief."

Lalique licked his lips—and collapsed. "Yes, I knew it was Jeffrey behind The Plaza robbery! Yes, I *saw* him!"

Jimmy snapped, "And you withheld the information!"

Lalique shrank. "I was afraid! I saw Jeffrey with that thief *before* the party, but I didn't know what it meant until after Victor was dead and The Plaza robbed! Later, I was too scared to talk, and then Jeffrey was killed, and I realized that someone else was involved in Victor's murder! Someone else who might kill *me!* I didn't know who, so . . ."

"Hold it!" Jimmy said, thinking hard. "Jeffrey Lowman hired the heist men and the button man—but in cahoots with someone else. He wanted Cosmo dead, and the ledger safe—but someone else wanted the ledger, too, maybe to use as blackmail on Lowman. So the other party tried to double-cross Lowman by sending the button man to grab the ledger from the heist men. When the ledger wasn't there, the second party thought that Lowman had pulled his own double-cross—and killed Lowman!"

"Analysis of son is correct—up to point," Chan said softly. "Remember, Jeffrey Lowman hire Plaza thieves *before* party. But Lowman know of ledger only when Victor Cosmo announce at party. Or so it seem. But Lowman *must* have known of ledger before it was announced. Only way that could have been was for his accomplice to have told him of existence of deadly ledger before Victor Cosmo did."

Chan looked around at all of them. "Victor Cosmo was very intelligent man, if not talented. A student of human nature. To dominate so many people, must have known science of human personality well. Was very sure he *knew* people he dealt with. And that was fatal mistake—Victor Cosmo was so sure of his knowledge of people that he became arrogant—and blind—to danger around him."

Chan reached again into his pocket, took out the memo sheet with Jeffrey Lowman's doodles on it. "Today, I discover this paper made by Jeffrey Lowman on night of his death." Chan read the paper. " . . . *arrogant . . . arrogant . . . both of us . . . blind idiots . . . must tell . . . must . . .*"

Chan laid the paper down, then looked up. "Jeffrey

Lowman realize too late he made same mistake as Victor Cosmo—both underestimate murderer, both so arrogant of own powers of judgment they fail to see true danger in killer. Fail to see real motive."

"Real motive?" Jimmy said. "But, Pop . . ."

"Killer," Chan said, "must be one who knew of death-threat tape *before* played at party."

He looked at Lorraine MacCall and Winston Cleaver. The actress paled, opened her mouth to speak, then closed it. Winston Cleaver only smiled, a thin, sharklike smile.

"Killer," Chan said, "must also be one who knew of existence of ledger *before* revealed at party."

He looked at Lalique. The little painter shrank back.

"Killer," Chan said, "is one Jeffrey Lowman was so sure he could use and outwit, but who outwitted him because Lowman made vast underestimation."

They all looked at each other, each accusing. Natalie stared at them all in a kind of rage.

"Killer," Chan said, "is one close to Victor Cosmo—so close as to be unseen like upstairs maid, an ornament of no concern to arrogant philanthropist, and one who could grant easiest access to bathroom to hired killer!"

Chan turned to Natalie.

"Alas, Natalie," he said simply. "You are murderer!"

28

The dazzling blonde model sat unmoving in her mourning clothes. She shook her lovely head and smiled sadly.

"I . . . I know this is a trick, Mr. Chan," she said in a halting voice. "You're trapping the real murderer, but I'm not smart enough to know how to help you."

"Regret," Chan said, equally sadly, "but is not trick. You are only one close enough to arrange death of Victor Cosmo, and at same time have no fear of secrets revealed by ledger after his death! Only you hide hatred of Cosmo so well that he fail to be on guard near you. Only you have real motives."

"What motives, Pop?" Jimmy said, watching the blonde.

"Natalie had no wish to be abused by Cosmo as she was, or discarded by arrogant male in a few years which was inevitable. Once discarded, she would have had no money and no means of support. Ledger would be source of income if in her hands—blackmail other guests, or sell to highest bidder. Of all guests that night, Natalie was only one who could be real winner by death of Victor Cosmo."

"You mean," Jimmy said, staring at Natalie, "she found out about the death threat, and about the ledger, before the party? She saw a real golden opportunity. She told Lowman about the ledger, got him to hire the heist men and the button man, and then double-crossed him? She got the button man to kill Cosmo, to kill the Plaza thieves for the ledger, and then to kill Lowman when she thought he still had the ledger?"

"All true, except do not think she *told* Jeffrey Lowman of her plan to murder Cosmo. Suggest she told Lowman only that goal was theft of ledger, fool him, too," Chan said. "Only Natalie could have known of *both* death-threat tape *and* ledger before party. Unsuspecting Cosmo play tape before her the day before, and mention precaution of ledger in her presence."

In the silence that descended on the room, the way it had on the night of Victor Cosmo's party when he told of what he knew and the precautions he had taken, Natalie smiled.

"But you have no proof at all, Mr. Chan," she said. "I'm not smart, but I know none of that would stand up in a court."

Jimmy and Norbitz looked at each other. Chan only nodded as if she were quite correct.

"Modern policeman son object to old-fashioned methods of venerable Honolulu detective," Chan said. "Gathering together of forewarned suspects of police, in empty house announced to all in advance, is ancient cliché. All forget that old methods and clichés once had good reason to be used. Were necessary in time before scientific means of detection were available, before police had men and means to secure hard proof. Used then because only sure way to get proof of guilt was to have murderer reveal self by making mistake that trap self!"

He frowned in the bright sitting room. "Such was situation in this case—no proof. Therefore, Chan forced to resort to old method, use self as bait to trap killer. Killer very good to oblige." His voice was dry. "Almost too good."

Now Chan glared at Natalie. "Recent attempt on life of Chan in this house prove you are murderer—even in court."

"I never . . ." Natalie began.

"Useless," Chan snapped. "Who else know this house so well could trap Chan in dark? Who else need to use method of wire through door because does not have strength to attack except in such a way that renders superior strength of Chan useless? Who else now have key to pantry door in purse!"

Natalie jumped up. Jimmy was quicker. He wrenched the purse from her hands, opened it, and dumped out the contents.

The old-fashioned door key lay among the compact, lipstick and Kleenex.

"Only key to pantry door in house, I have checked," Chan said. "Mistake of reflex in haste to escape—automatically drop key in purse. Observed in purse by many witnesses who will speak in court—also by two police officers."

Natalie seemed to freeze. Everyone watched her. Then, without warning, she snatched a long, steel letter-opener from a delicate writing desk, and rushed at Chan. The wicked knife swung up in her small hand.

Norbitz stepped out, hesitated a split-second, then hit the girl flush on the jaw with all his two-hundred-and-twenty pounds of muscle.

The 'Thwock!' echoed through the sitting room, and the slender model went down like a pole-axed cow, out cold on the elegant carpet, her arms and legs spread-eagled in smooth expanses of soft, clear flesh.

Norbitz blinked. "Jesus! I never hit a woman before."

"How was it?" Jimmy said, grinning.

"Not bad," Norbitz said in wonder. "Not bad at all."

No one moved to revive the fallen Natalie. For several long minutes they all just sat there. Then Lalique stood, and walked to where the black ledger lay. He picked it up, opened it, and then whirled on Chan in disbelief.

"Why—it's blank! There's nothing in the ledger!"

Chan shrugged. "Simple matter to buy ledger in shop, send to myself with Victor Cosmo's name on it, so that any guilty watching would think I had real ledger."

He looked down at the groaning Natalie. "Seem to work."

Three days later, his vacation over, Charlie Chan stepped from The Walforf-Astoria elevator into the lobby. He was accompanied by Jimmy and the bellhops carrying his luggage, and he held his covered birdcage. He stopped to stare at a scene going on at the main desk.

Lalique, dressed now completely in red, stood at the desk with two women. The women, one on each arm, were dressed identically! In every detail of face, makeup, hair and clothes, they were twins—except that one was a full thirty years older than the other!

Lalique was drawn up to his full height in front of the gaping desk clerk.

"Who . . . who shall I say wants Mr. Chan?"

"Who?" Lalique cried. "My card!"

He extended a small, white business card. The clerk blinked at it incredulously.

"But . . . ," he stammered, "there's nothing on this card!"

"Lalique," the little artist said, "needs no introduction!"

Chan and Jimmy walked through the lobby toward the desk. Lalique saw them. Beaming, he dismissed the desk clerk with a wave, and advanced on Chan with his two escorts.

"Mr. Lalique," Chan said, bowing. "A red period, I see?"

"Of course!" The painter smiled his Cheshire cat smile. He observed Jimmy staring at his two women. He pointed to the younger woman. "This is *Before.*" He pointed to the older woman. "And this is *After!*"

"Some," he said, "think they are two people, but they are not! I know, because I have created them! My ultimate achievement—human sculpture!"

Even Chan was taken aback. "Most extraordinary."

"But," Lalique beamed, "I have not come to have you fawn at *my* feet, worthy as I am." He grinned. "I have come, Mr. Chan, to thank you for keeping my name out of the papers in this sad affair."

"Thanks are not required," Chan dismissed it.

"And," Lalique went on, suddenly serious, "to ask for an important piece of information for two others besides myself. Mr. Chan, where is Victor's real ledger? If you have it now, can we prevail on you to destroy . . . "

"No," Chan said, his voice quiet. "Because there is no ledger, Mr. Lalique, there never was! Man like Victor Cosmo could not allow existence of book as damaging to himself as to others. He simply manipulated you all with nothing more than an invention. Murders all done for book that never exists!" Chan sighed. "Small point Natalie fail to know. All her murders without chance of profit from start. All wasted."

Lalique blinked. "No ledger?"

"Victor Cosmo's trick, cost many lives—including his own," Chan said. "Now must catch plane. Will remember Lalique with pleasure."

Chan and Jimmy walked across the lobby, and out to a waiting taxi. As Chan got in, Jimmy glanced back to where Lalique was strutting out of the hotel with his bizarre women.

"That guy," Jimmy said, "is a real coconut."

Chan peered out of the taxi. "Eccentricity often brother of genius. But . . . yes, a coconut!"

Jimmy laughed. "Have a safe trip home, Pop. Next vacation, keep out of trouble."

"Goal of even detective's life," Chan said. "Please to write mother perhaps three times a year, if duties at places like Serpent's Eye allow time." The taxi pulled away from the curb in front of the elegant old hotel. Chan leaned out, called back, "And cut your hair!"

Jimmy waved, and the taxi was gone.